Leigh Hunt

A Jar of Honey from Mount Hybla

Leigh Hunt

A Jar of Honey from Mount Hybla

ISBN/EAN: 9783337288778

Printed in Europe, USA, Canada, Australia, Japan

Cover: Foto ©Andreas Hilbeck / pixelio.de

More available books at **www.hansebooks.com**

A JAR OF HONEY

FROM

MOUNT HYBLA

BY LEIGH HUNT

ILLUSTRATED BY RICHARD DOYLE

A NEW EDITION

LONDON

SMITH, ELDER, & CO., 15 WATERLOO PLACE

1883

TO

HORACE SMITH,

WHO, THOUGH HE SUPPRESSES THE PASTORALS WHICH HE WROTE

IN HIS YOUTH,

.

WILL RETAIN AS LONG AS HE LIVES,

A HEART OPEN TO EVERY NATURAL AND NOBLE IMPRESSION,

THESE PAGES,

WITHOUT HIS KNOWLEDGE, BUT CONFIDING IN HIS INDULGENCE,

Are Inscribed,

BY HIS EVER GRATEFUL AND AFFECTIONATE FRIEND,

LEIGH HUNT.

CONTENTS.

CHAPTER IV.

THEOCRITUS.

CHAPTER V.

THEOCRITUS.—(CONCLUDED.)

CHAPTER VI.

NORMAN TIMES—LEGEND OF KING ROBERT.

CHAPTER VII.

ITALIAN AND ENGLISH PASTORAL.

CHAPTER VIII.

ENGLISH PASTORAL—(CONTINUED); AND SCOTCH PASTORAL.

CHAPTER IX.

ENGLISH PASTORAL.—(Concluded.)

CHAPTER X.

RETURN TO SICILY AND MOUNT ÆTNA.

CHAPTER XI.

BEES.

CHAPTER XII.

MISCELLANEOUS FEELINGS RESPECTING SICILY, ITS MUSIC, ITS RELIGION, AND ITS MODERN POETRY.

OVERFLOWINGS OF THE JAR.

LIST OF ILLUSTRATIONS

DESIGNED AND DRAWN ON WOOD BY RICHARD DOYLE.

CHRISTMAS AND ITALY;

OR

A PREFATORY ESSAY, SHOWING THE EXTREME FITNESS OF THIS BOOK FOR THE SEASON.

I N one of the volumes of that celebrated French publi-
cation, the *Almanach des Gourmands*, which sounds
the depth of the merit of soups, and decides on the dis-
tracting claims of the most affinitive relishes, there is
a frontispiece presenting to the respectful eyes of the
reader a "Jury of Tasters." They form a board of
elderly gentlemen with the most thoughtful faces, and
are in the act of chewing each his mouthful, and
profoundly ruminating on its pretensions. Having
seen but this single volume of the work, and that only
for a short time (which we mention with becoming

1

regret), we are not qualified to report its verdicts; but one of them made an impression on us not to be forgotten. It ran as follows :—"With this sauce a man might eat his father."

Now, far are we, in the most ambitious moments of our honey-making, from aspiring at a judgment upon us like that ;—sad evidence of the excesses of imagination into which the most serious intellects may be transported, in consequence of giving way to their appetites. One of the especial parts of our vocation is to draw sweet out of bitter ; and the only association of ideas which these unfilial sages brought to our mind, was that of an equally searching, but far nobler set of judges, who, when this our Honey first made its appearance at the periodical table of Mr. Ainsworth, and was thence diffused over the country, exclaimed from all quarters, after the most benignant meditation, "With this sauce a man might swallow some of the bitterest morsels of life." "This is the condiment to sweeten every man's daily bread." "There is the right Christian aroma in the sacrificial part of the offering of these dulcitudes."

We blush, of course, with the requisite modesty in repeating these approvals ; and, indeed, should blush a great deal more if we thought that the contents of our Jar (as far as they originate with ourselves) had any merit

beyond such as might easily be competed with by thousands throughout the land, upon the strength of their
own thoughts and good-will, assisted by a little reading and cheerfulness ; but the truth is, that our friends
in Cornhill, having purchased the stock in consequence
of those approvals, and thinking it worth their while,
after it had been clarified and augmented, to put it into
elegant vehicles of their own, and so qualify it to be made
into Christmas presents, we are desirous to show how fit
it is for that purpose; nay, how emphatically it would have
been so considered in the "good old Christmas times."

It is true, that besides the good old Christmas
times, there are such things as good *new* Christmas
times ; and in respect to the great object of both, we
are heartily of opinion that the latter far surpass the
former, and that no literary fare for the season ever
came up to the substantial as well as exquisite food set
forth for us in the pages of *Chimes* and *Christmas
Carols*. They are nectar and ambrosia for the spirit
in the humblest shapes of the flesh. They are the
sermons of the morning rescued from the dead letter of
mere assent and custom, reproduced with all the allure-
ments of wit and pathos, and made contributory to the
greatest practical workings of the time. And the time
has no greater glory than the fact of the conversion of
satire itself to a beneficent spirit, which (with a few

occasional deviations, that must be pardoned for habit's sake) it obviously and largely possesses, and which it will complete ere long, by an impartiality towards every rank and description of men.

These exceptions to our claims being admitted, we shall grow bold on the strength of our candour; and aver, that our Jar of Honey is eminently suited to almost all other old Christmas associations (of an unvulgar order), while at the same time it does not omit, if it does not prominently put forth, this modern one of the right Christian spirit; as indeed, by the favour of the critics, has already been noticed. Christmas amusements of old were a mixture of poetry, piety, revelry, superstition, story-telling, and masquing, particularly Pagan and Arcadian masquing; and here you have them all. But they were not confined to these. At no time does talk run freer on all subjects than at Christmas, because at no time are the animal spirits set more at liberty; and hence no topic is baulked if it come uppermost, any more than it is in these pages. And as to the foreign part of our title, when Shakspeare wrote his *Winter's Tale* (and a Winter's Tale was emphatically a Christmas Tale) he laid the scene of it in the same country as that of our little Jar. Shakspeare's Christmas Tale is a Sicilian tale, and it presents the same mixture as we do, of old Sicilian story and English pastoral. To be exclusively English was never the con-templation of any Christmas talk. No later than the other day, Coleridge wrote a play in professed imitation of the *Winter's Tale*. He calls it " Zapolya, a *Christmas Tale*," and the scene is laid in Illyria ; which, by the way, is that of Shakspeare's *Twelfth-Night*, another play of the season, for Twelfth-Night is included in Christmas. Indeed, if you would banish foreign matters from Christmas, you must banish Christmas itself. You must sweep away mince-pies, with their currants from Greece, their cloves and mace from the Spice Islands, and their peel of lemon from *Sicily*. You must abolish your plum-pudding, with its raisins from Malaga, your boar's head from Germany, chestnuts from Spain and France, oranges from Portugal, wines every one of them, except British, all your hot pickles, all your teas and coffees, your very twelfth-cake with its sugar : nay, even the name of the season, to say nothing of things too reverend to be specified. You would not have a ma-hogany table to dine upon. Sixpence would not be left you to buy a cigar, nor a cigar to be bought ; and if you wished to console yourself with singing a carol, ten to one but the tune would be taken out of your mouth, being found to belong to Pergolese or Palestrina, or some other Italian inventor of the phrases of melody.

Italian ! Why, Italy will be talked about this

Christmas at half the tables in England, with the Pope and Mr. Cobden at its head ; and we think we see our little Blue Jar the more valued accordingly. Mr. Cobden has returned from Italy, brimful, as such a man ought to be, of its beauties and merits. He himself will talk plentifully about it ; and others will talk, because he has talked already. The Duke of Devonshire has been in Italy. Lord John has an Envoy in Italy. Every reigning circle of private and public life has had its representative visitor in that country. Everybody, indeed, may be said to visit it every day in the newspapers, to see how the Pope and Reform are going on ; poor Sicily has been in trouble with its " Captain Romeo " (strange link of times past and present) ; and Mr. Cobden has the magnanimity to express his regret that he had not made himself a master, when he was young, of the language of the beautiful peninsula.

Now, one of the great objects of the present writer, for many years past, has been to lure his readers into the love of other languages, particularly of this most beautiful of them all. It is for this reason he has scarcely ever quoted the most trivial expression from any one of them without giving a version of it ; knowing well, how many intelligent men there are who would enjoy the original, if they knew it, far better than many an accidental scholar, and who are therefore willing to have the least glimpse of it afforded them. It has been well said, that "mankind will cease to quarrel with one another, when they understand one another." Mr. Cobden, in his entertaining and instructive speech at the Manchester Athenæum, has told us how he was struck with this conviction during his tour. But he arrived at it before, by the intuition of a happy nature. Why, for his own delight, does he not make himself a master of the language he so admires? He is a reader by the fireside; and one hour's reading, *per diem*, would render such a man more intimate with it in the course of a year than nine-tenths of its masters in England. But perhaps he is such. At all events, he may have become acquainted with it sufficiently for enjoyment; as much, for instance, as ourselves; more so, if he speaks it; for though we read, well enough, most of the languages that we translate, we can speak them no better than just to make our way through Italy and France. We mention this, partly that we may not seem to know more than we do, and partly to encourage others to learn. A little hearty love is better in this, as in all other cases, than a heap of indifferent knowledge. We are ashamed to say, that we know less of Greek, in one sense of the word, than we did when young, and are obliged to look out more words in the dictionary; for to a dictionary we are still forced to resort, though we love the language next to Italian, and hold it in higher admiration. But then we know our ignorance better than we did at that time ; are more aware of beauties to be enjoyed, and nice meanings to be discovered ; and the consequence is, that whenever we undertake to translate a passage from Greek, we take our love on one side of us, and our dictionary on the other, and before we set about it, make a point of sifting every possible meaning and root of meaning, not excepting those in words the most familiar to us, in order that not an atom of the writer's intention may be missed. We do not say, of course, that we always succeed in detecting it; but it is not for want of painstaking.

The labour we delight in, physicks pain.

Now by a like respect for the good old maxim of "slow and sure," and by dint of doing a little, or even a very little, every day, there is no lover of poetry and beauty who in the course of a few months might not be as deep as a bee in some of the sweetest flowers of other languages; and it is for readers of this sort that we have not only translated and commented on Greek and other passages in the book before us, but in some instances given intimations of the spirit in which we have studied them ;—being anxious to allure to the study such as can find time for it, and to give some little taste of their exquisiteness to those who cannot. For all sorts of benefits lie in a knowledge of languages, both to men out of the world and men in it;—all additions to the stock of profit and pleasure,—to the certainty of knowing (as the phrase is) "what to be at" on occasions where profitable information is required; of not losing any advantage, either of relative or of positive gain; of growing superior to debasing fears and to ignorant and inhuman assumptions; and above all, of assisting the great cause of the advancement and mutual intercourse of all men, which shall put an end to narrow-minded ideas of profit and loss, and open up that moral, and intellectual, and cordial as well as commercial Free Trade, without which we should remain little better for ever than a parcel of ill-taught children, willing, if not able, to cheat one another in corners. But all this cannot be done, unless knowledge and taste go hand-in-hand; or, in other words, unless we learn to perceive the finally pleasurable, as well as the intermediately profitable; otherwise, when we come to the end of our gain, we shall be but at the beginning of a sense of our unfitness to enjoy it; and this, too, after missing a thousand graces by the way. Supposing health, for instance, and other favourable circumstances to have been on a par, which of any two men in the age of Shakspeare was the more capable of enjoying the

whole round of his Christmas holidays,—he who had
plenty of money to disburse for them, but no taste for
their plays and pageants beyond what was shared by
everybody who had eyes and ears; or he who understood
all the beauties of their imagery and their allusions;
who saw their colours with the eye of a painter, and
heard their words with the apprehension of a poet; to
whom the music was not a mere prettiness to patronise,
or movement to beat time to, but an interweaving of
shapes of grace and circles of harmony; to whom gods
indeed descended from heaven, and nymphs brought
back ages of gold; to whom terror itself was but a
passing phase of the operation of good; and by, as well
as for, whom, some justice, however small, was thus
done to that magnificence of sight and suggestiveness
with which heaven has adorned the universe, and that
tendency to hope the best of all things which no seem-
ing contradiction can do away?   To feel thus is not
only to be able to endure the perplexities presented to
the mind by Christmas itself, its poor, and its polemics,
but to pass the "flaming bounds" of telescope and
microscope, and repose in serenities beyond the finite.

We have been led into an unexpected strain of
enthusiasm and exaltation; but this is as natural to
the season as a church-organ, or as the memory of the
Sermon on the Mount. Christmas sees fair play to all

reasonable moods of mind, the cheerful being pre-
dominant, as the height of reason. After church comes
an interval, and after the interval dinner, which is a
mixture of the serious and the lively; solid as to the
beef and pudding, but light as regards the laughter and
the whipped syllabub. Then ensue pastimes for a
succession of days, including Twelfth-Day, with reading
of books in the morning, and cards and conversation at
night; the young chiefly being the players at the once
courtly games of forfeits and "Bob," and the old the
performers at whist and the wine-bottle. Our modern
Christmas entertainments will not bear comparison for
vigour of enjoyment with those of our ancestors before
Cromwell's time, either out of doors or in. They have
never recovered the blow given them by the invidious
heaviness of the Puritans. But to make amends, we
have refined on some of their pleasures; have multiplied
others, as in the case of the theatres; and we possess
an overflow of their own favourite reading, such as their
poets might have envied us. Rare manuscripts have
been set free in popular editions; we read the stories
which our ancestors used to tell, with thousands of new
novels to boot; Christmas alone brings with it a shower
of gorgeous and sometimes admirable publications, as
if flowers came pouring down with its snow; and in
fine, beloved reader, here is our (and your) Jar of

Honey, full of the sweet Paganism that was dear to the Shakspeares and Miltons, of the Pastoral which they loved also, of the right Christmas adventures of *King Robert of Sicily*, (which they perused under another title in the *Gesta Romanorum*,) of all sorts of good Italianate things, (then, as now, looked upon with wonderful curiosity and respect;) and finally, if loving wishes deceive us not, a sample and prelibation of that quintessential extract of the spirit of Christianity itself, the effect of which is to take away all doubt respecting the celestial balsam, and to make men wonder how they came to mistake for it anything containing the least taste of the fiery, the bitter, or the sour.

If the great and good Pope now reigning (for such he seems to be, in spite of some official drawbacks) has goodness enough to feel the wish, and could ever find greatness enough in him to dare to venture the act, of summoning a new Council of the Church, that should set on its altar this pure and unadulterated attraction of all hearts, instead of the unseemly manufactures of Councils of Trent and Priests of St. Januarius, he would give St. Peter's its only final chance of continuing to be the throne of the Christian world, and of flourishing under the sweet and only desirable blossom, that shall have done some day for ever with its thorns.

But to return from these altitudes. The story of

King Robert, we beg leave to say, is an especial delight of our soul, and gave us some exquisite moments in the writing. How came Shakspeare to let such a subject escape him? or Beaumont and Fletcher? or Decker? or any of the great and loving spirits that abounded in that romantic age? It was extant in manuscript; it abounded, under another name, in print; it presented the most striking dramatic points; extremes of passion were in the characters; pride and its punishment were in it; humility and its reward; a court, a chapel, an angel; pomp, music, satire, buffoonery, sublimity, tears. O Fate! give us a dozen years more life, and a lift in our faculties, immense; and let us try still if even our own verses cannot do something with it.

There is not, we will venture to say, a single portion of our Jar, which does not contain appropriate reading for Christmas.

The first chapter concerns the *Arabian Nights*; and every little boy knows that the *Arabian Nights* are reading for all seasons, particularly holidays.

The second chapter is full of the Fairy Tales of Antiquity; things which people used to relate round their fires during the ancient Saturnalia, just as our ancestors used to do at Christmas, and as boys read them still. And the Saturnalia were not only, to the ancients, what the Christmas holidays are to us, but the veritable parents and progenitors of those holidays, as every antiquary knows. It is doubtful whether Macrobius, who wrote a *Saturnalia*, or Christmas Holiday Book, of his time, was a Pagan or a Christian; but, at all events, his book is full of every kind of miscellaneous reading and gossiping, from Scipio's Dream down to a scandalous anecdote and a disputed passage in Virgil. Such was the pastime, he tells us, at that season, of the best-informed circles at Rome.

Our third chapter contains, among other Saturnalian subjects, the story of the truly Christmas-like personage, Gellias, one of the wittiest and most hospitable of entertainers, a noble-hearted merchant-prince, who kept seven hundred gallons of wine in his house, and was famous for making his workmen happy.

Our fourth and fifth chapters, besides some Saturnalian stories, include an account of an ancient holiday, full of gossip, and show, and leafy boughs, together with a vast deal of Pastoral,—a summer recollection, to which Christmas has always been fond of reverting, at least in books and among the poets; probably on the principle of extremes meeting, and by a happy rule of contraries. It is observable how fond we are at Christmas of what our forefathers used to call " greens," that is to say, boughs and flowers and everything which can force the summer, as it were, to remain with us by our firesides.

The sixth chapter is our beloved subject, the story of King Robert aforesaid.

The seventh brings us, through Italian Pastoral, to the Christmas poetical entertainments of our ancestors.

In the eighth and ninth we are in the Old English Poetical Works. In the tenth at Mount Ætna with its stories. In the eleventh with the Bees. In the twelfth with the musical services of the Church, with cheerful picties of all sorts, and with the jovial Sicilian poet, Meli, one of the most universal of men.

Some persons have fancied that our book would be too learned! The most unlearned of such readers as we hope to possess will see what a notion this is, and to what plain English all our Greek and Latin has turned. We have the greatest contempt for learning, merely so called; together with the greatest respect for it when it sees through the dead letter of time and words into the spirit that concerns all ages and all descriptions of men. Every clever unlearned man in England, rich and poor, if we had the magic to do it, should be gifted to-morrow with all the learning that would adorn and endear his commerce to him, his agriculture, and the poorest flower-pot at his window. It would satisfy the longings that are born with such a man, and are natural to his powers; and would enable him, while he no longer envied such right parliamentary quoters of

Virgil as the Minister, or Macaulay, or Sir Robert, or Brougham, or Lord Ellesmere, or Lord Morpeth, or Fox, to laugh at such educated ignoramuses as A, B, and C, who, though the classics were beaten into their heads at school, have no more real taste for what they quote, than the wall has for the pictures that are hung upon it with nail and hammer.

Spirit is everything, and letter is nothing; except inasmuch as it is a vehicle for spirit. "The letter killeth, but the spirit giveth life." A learned quotation is as ridiculous in some people's mouths as a flower would be stuck in the mouth of a barber's block. What would the best claret be to one that could not perceive the odour of it? or the nicest of mince-pies, or college-puddings, to a mouth that had no taste? We are but dull ourselves in such matters (the more's the pity), and would fain share, when at table, the nicest discernments of sharp and sweet, possessed by the luckier palates around us; but we should only laugh at the poor devil of a pretender, who, with nothing but a palate of silver, and no taste at all, should affect to emulate the *Almanach des Gourmands*, and give his opinion of the contending sauces.

May we take, by the way, a Saturnalian liberty, and ask Members of Parliament why they quote no language but Latin, and in Latin no writers but Virgil and Horace?

We believe there is an occasional venture on Lucretius, and perhaps on Juvenal. Also, two passages from Ovid, one in praise of the Fine Arts, and another about preferring wrong pursuits to right perceptions. But French has lately been thought worthy of cultivation, even at public schools; almost every man of rank speaks it, and Italian is an ordinary accomplishment. Ariosto, Berni, and others, would supply an admirable crop of new parliamentary quotations; or, if there was a fear of the delicacy of the pronunciation, what hinders us from being refreshed with something from Molière, La Fontaine, Pascal, or a hundred other wits and thinkers among our gallant neighbours? New paths of quotation are due to railroads and Free Trade. There would be a sort of extension of Parliament itself into Paris and Rome, if we occasionally spoke the languages of those illustrious cities. France and Italy would be pleased; books benefited; politics smoothed; intercourse gladdened and enlarged. Even a bit of Greek might be ventured upon, if short and sweet; and Mr. Hume feel relieved in hearing (on the authority of the philosophic Hesiod) that "half" was "better than the whole" (πλέον ἥμισυ παντός).

The reverend maxim we have quoted respecting spirit and letter reminds us of a little Christmas story which has never been in print, and which, in accordance with

2

the season, we shall take this opportunity of relating. It was brought to our recollection by meeting with the following exquisite passage from Bacon :—

"As those wines which flow from the first treading of the grape are sweeter and better than those forced out by the press, which gives them the roughness of the husk and the stone, so are those doctrines best and sweetest which flow from *a gentle crush* of the Scriptures, and are not wrung into controversies and commonplaces."

That metaphor of the "husk" is one that has haunted us (so to speak), in connexion with the subject here alluded to, for half our lives; not suggested, we beg leave to say, by the great philosopher—(qualified though he be to suggest hundreds of things to us beyond our powers of origination)—but by the greater force of the necessity of admitting evil and reconciling it to good. And in that point of view the husk we allude to is nobler than Bacon's, or at least, than what seems to have been in his construction of the word; for we took it in the light of a necessary enclosure and safeguard of a future bud. But to drop this collateral reminiscence, and come to our story. It is entitled

THE ELIXIR AND THE VIALS.

Once on a time there was a dispute respecting the possession of a certain elixir, called by some Flower of

Thorn, by others Spirit of Lily, by others Spirit of Love, and by others various other names not necessary to mention, but agreed by all to produce the most wonderful effects on the mind, of peace and benevolence. The parties who laid claim to the glory and emoluments of this possession, said it was kept in a particular kind of vial distinguishable from every other, and belonging exclusively to one single proprietor; and each claimant declared, nay swore, that he was that one. Indeed, it was remarkable, that for persons valuing themselves on the possession of an essence, or spirit, producing such gentle effects, they were, most of them, wonderfully given to swearing, not hesitating to use the most extraordinary oaths, both in assertion of their own claims, and in condemnation of those of the rest. One of these gentlemen, holding up his vial, which was a very pretty thing to look at, exclaimed that every man might be, —— nay, was —— (we do not like to repeat the word), who did not see plainly that that was the only spirit. Another uttered the very same threats, though he held up a vial of a totally different appearance. The case was the same with a third, a fourth, and a fifth, nay, with a fiftieth. There was nothing to be seen but a flourishing of vials, and nothing to be heard but a storm of voices. At length, from words (as might be expected of such words) they proceeded to blows; and what was

very astonishing, they were so moved and provoked out
of their wits as to convert their respective vials into
weapons of offence, and so absolutely endeavour to fight
it out with the fragile materials.

The consequences may be guessed. Not only were
heads broken, but the vials also; and not only did the
spirit in the vials evaporate, but by the fury of the combatants, both before and after the breakage, it became
manifest that no such thing as a spirit producing the
effects they pretended, had been in the vials at all.

The scene ended with the laughter of the spectators;
and worse consequences might have ensued, but for the
appearance of a third set of persons bringing forward
another vial. It was totally unlike all the former, except in one part of it; and this part, which was of the
real crystal which the others only pretended to be, was
said to contain, and did absolutely contain, the veritable
peace-making elixir, as was proved by a very simple but
incontrovertible circumstance; namely, the peace-making itself. The proprietors neither swore, nor threatened,
nor fought, nor tried to identify the vial with its contents.
They proved the effect of those contents upon themselves
by the friendliest behaviour towards all parties present;
and though they had a long and difficult task to induce
their rivals to taste it, yet no sooner had they done so,
than the whole place became a scene of the most

enchanting reasonableness and serenity. Everybody embraced his neighbour with the kindest words, and the combatants themselves did not scruple to wonder how they could have missed perceiving the presence of an odour so sweet, so unadulterated, so unquestionable, so tranquillizing, and so divine.

This story is not so good as Robert of Sicily, or as one that we shall relate presently; but it is not inferior to either in the conclusions that may be drawn from it; and assuredly (except from the edification to be drawn from scandals themselves) it is better than the histories of all the controversies that have agitated the schools of East and West. As to that of the Sicilian King, we are so fond of it that we cannot help taking the opportunity it affords us of thanking the young artist who has illustrated it, and who, after distinguishing himself with the public for his humour, has shown in these pages so much promise of a more serious order. He has not chosen to give his angel much bodily substance; perhaps the better to intimate the spiritual nature of the being, and give the more supernatural solemnity to his departure. But nobody can doubt the solidity which accompanies the grace of King Robert; and the royal penitent has been judiciously reinvested with the garb of his rank, the moment he resumes his personal identity. We must be allowed also to express our sense of the Poussin-like figure of Polyphemus at page 88, with his lumpish but not ungraceful shoulders (fit symbols of the heaviness of his mind) ; nor can we omit noticing the truly pastoral grace and simplicity of the Shepherdess at page 71, who is leading a flock full of nature and movement ; and we are particularly thankful for the fidelity with which the artist has transferred to paper the sensitive and benignant profile of the Sicilian poet Meli, a cast of a medallion of whose likeness we have the good fortune to possess. Mr. Doyle, throughout his drawings, has shown great attention to costume and other such proprieties ; one of the evidences of that regard for truth, without which no art of any kind can ever come to perfection.

We shall conclude this article with a brief Christmas story to which there is an allusion in the one above mentioned, and which we hold to be worth, at least, some nine hundred and forty thousand sermons. It is entitled

THE ELEVEN COMMANDMENTS.

A certain bishop who lived some hundred years ago, and who was very unlike what is reported of her Majesty's new almoner ; also very unlike the Christian bishops of old, before titles were invented for them ; very unlike Fenelon too, who nevertheless had plenty of titles ; very

unlike St. Francis de Sales, who was for talking nothing
but "roses;" very unlike St. Vincent de Paul, who
founded the Sisterhood of Charity; very unlike Rundle,
who "had a heart," and Berkeley, who had "every virtue
under heaven," and that other exquisite bishop (we
blush to have forgotten his name), who was grieved to
find that he had a hundred pounds at his banker's when
the season had been so bad for the poor;—this highly
unresembling bishop, who, nevertheless, was like too
many of his brethren,—that is to say, in times past (for
there is no bishop, now, at least in any quarter of
England, who is not remarkable for meekness, and does
not make a point of turning his right cheek to be smitten,
the moment you have smitten his left);—this unepisco-
pal, and yet not impossible bishop, we say, was once ac-
costed, during a severe Christmas, by a Parson Adams
kind of inferior clergyman, and told a long story of the
wants of certain poor people, of whose cases his lordship
was unaware. What the dialogue was, which led to the
remark we are about to mention, the reporters of the circumstance do not appear to have ascertained; but it seems
that, the representations growing stronger and stronger
on one side, and the determination to pay no attention to
them acquiring proportionate vigour on the other, the
clergyman was moved to tell the bishop that his lordship did not understand his " eleven commandments."

"Eleven commandments!" cried the bishop; "why, fellow, you are drunk. Who ever heard of an eleventh commandment? Depart, or you shall be put in the stocks."

"Put thine own pride and cruelty in the stocks," retorted the good priest, angered beyond his Christian patience, and preparing to return to the sufferers for whom he had pleaded in vain. "I say there are *eleven* commandments, *not* ten, and that it were well for such flocks as you govern, if it were added, as it ought to be, to the others over the tables in church. Does your lordship remember—do you in fact know anything at all of Him who came on earth to do good to the poor and woeful, and who said, 'Behold, I give unto you a *new* commandment, LOVE ONE ANOTHER?'"

A

JAR OF HONEY FROM MOUNT HYBLA.

CHAPTER I.

INTRODUCTORY.

A BLUE JAR FROM SICILY,
AND A BRASS JAR
FROM THE "ARABIAN
NIGHTS;" AND WHAT
CAME OUT OF EACH.

PASSING one day
by the shop of
Messrs. Fortnum and
Mason in Piccadilly, we
beheld in the window a
little blue jar, labelled,
"Sicilian Honey."—It
was a jar of very humble
pretensions, if estimated
according to its price in
the market. Perhaps it
might have been worth,
as a piece of ware, about

threepence ; and, contents and all, its price did not
exceed eighteenpence. People who condescend to look
at nothing but what is costly, and who, being worth a
vast deal of money at their bankers', are not aware that
they are poor devils as men, would have infallibly
despised it ; or, at the very utmost, they would have
associated it in their minds with nothing but the con-
fectioner or the store-room. On the other hand, it might
have reminded a Cavendish or a Gower of his Titians
and Correggios ; and a Rogers would surely have
looked twice at it, for the sake of his Stothard and
his *Italy*.   And the poet and the noble dukes would
have been right, not only in the spirit of their
recollections, but to the very letter ; for the deep
beautiful blue was the same identical blue, the result of
the same mineral, by which such an effect is retained in
old pictures ; and the shape of the jar was as classical
as that of many a vase from the antique.   Antiquity,
indeed, possessed an abundance of precisely such jars.
Furthermore, when you held the jar in the sun, a spot
of insufferable radiance came in the middle of its cheek,
like a very laugh of light. Then it contained honey—
a thing which strikes the dullest imaginations with a
sense of sweetness and the flowers ; and in addition to
the word " honey " outside, was the word " Sicilian "
—a very musical and meminiscent word.

Now in consequence of this word "Sicilian," by a certain magical process, not unlike that of the seal of the mighty Solomon, which could put an enormous quantity of spirit into a wonderfully small vessel, the inside of our blue jar (for be sure we bought it) became enriched, beyond its honey, to an extent which would appear incredible to any readers but such as we have the honour to address, doubtless the most intelligent of their race.

To introduce it, however, even to them, in a manner befitting their judgment, it is proper that we call to their recollection the history of a previous jar of their acquaintance, to which the foregoing paragraph contains an allusion.

They will be pleased to call to mind that eighteen hundred years after the death of Solomon, and during the reign of the King of the Black Isles, who was (literally) half petrified by the conduct of his wife, a certain fisherman, after throwing his nets to no purpose, and beginning to be in despair, succeeded in catching a jar of brass. The brass, to be sure, seemed the only valuable thing about the jar; but the fisherman thought he could, at least, sell it for old metal. Finding, however, that it was very heavy, and furthermore closed with a seal, he wisely resolved to open it first, and see what could be got out of it.

He therefore took a knife—(we quote from Mr. Torrens's *Arabian Nights*, not out of disregard for that other
interesting version by our excellent friend Mr. Lane,
but we have lent his first volume, and Galland does not
contain the whole passage; he seems to have thought
it would frighten the ladies of his day)—the fisherman,
therefore, "took a knife," says Mr. Torrens, and "worked
at the tin cover till he had separated it from the jar ;
and he put it down by his side on the ground.   Then
he shook the jar, to tumble out whatever might be
in it, and found in it not a thing.   So he marvelled
with extreme amazement.   But presently there came
out of the jar a vapour, and it rose up towards the
heavens, and reached along the face of the earth; and
after this, the vapour reached its height, and condensed,
and became compact, and waved tremulously, and
became an Ufreet (evil spirit), his head in the clouds,
and his foot on the soil, *his head like a dome, his hand
like a harrow,* his two legs like pillars, his mouth like
a pit, *his teeth like large stones,* and his nostrils like
basins, and his eyes were two lamps, *austere and
louring.*   Now, when the fisherman *saw that Ufreet,*
his muscles shivered, and his teeth chattered, *and his
palate was dried up,* and he knew not where he was."

This, by the way, is a fine horrible picture, and very
like an Ufreet; as anybody must know, who is intimate

with that delicate generation. We are acquainted with
nothing that beats it in its way, except the description
of another in the *Bahar Danush*, who, while sleeping
on the ground, draws the pebbles towards him with his
breath, and sends them back again as it goes forth;
though a little further on, in the *Arabian Nights*, is
an Ufreet of a most accomplished ugliness—namely,
"*the lord of all that is detestable to look at!*" What a
jurisdiction! And the "lord" too! Fancy a viscount
of that description.

The fright and astonishment conceived by the fisherman at the taste thus given him of this highly concen-
trated spirit of *Jinn* (for such is the generic Eastern
term for the order to which the Ufreet belongs) were
not, however, the only things he got out of his jar. An
incarceration of eighteen hundred years at the bottom
of the ocean, under the seal of the mighty Solomon, had
taught its prisoner a little more respect for that kind of
detainder than he had been wont to exhibit; the fisherman exacted from him an oath of good treatment in
the event of his being set free; and the consequence
was, that after the adventures of the coloured fish, of the
appearance of the lady out of the wall, and of the semi-
petrifaction of the King of the Black Islands with his
lonely voice, our piscatory friend is put in possession of
his majesty's throne. So here is an Ufreet as high as

the clouds, fish that would have delighted Titian, (they
were blue, white, yellow, and red,) a lady, full-dressed,
issuing out of a kitchen wall, a king half-turned to
stone by his wife, a throne given to a fisherman, and
half-a-dozen other phenomena, *all resulting from one
poor brazen jar*, into which when the fisherman first
looked, he saw nothing in it.

> A brass jar by the ocean's brim,
> A yellow brass jar was to him,
> And it was nothing more.

Now we might have expected as little from our
earthen jar, as the future monarch did from his jar of
metal, had not some circumstances in our life made us
acquainted with the philosophy and occult properties
of jars; but such having been the case, no lover of the
Arabian Nights (which is another term for a reader
with a tendency to the universal) will be surprised at
the quantity and magnitude of the things that arose
before our eyes out of the little blue jar in the window
of Messrs. Fortnum and Mason.

"Sicilian Honey."—We had no sooner read those
words, than Theocritus rose before us, with all his
poetry.

Then Sicily arose—the whole island—particularly
Mount Ætna. Then Mount Hybla, with its bees.

Then Rucellai (the Italian poet of the bees) and his

predecessor Virgil, and Acis and Galatea, and Polyphemus, a pagan Ufreet, but mild—mitigated by love, as
Theocritus has painted him.

Then the *Odyssey*, with the giant in his fiercer days,
before he had sown his wild rocks; and the Sirens; and
Scylla and Charybdis; and Ovid; and Alpheus and
Arethusa; and Proserpina, and the Vale of Enna—
names, which bring before us whatever is blue in skies,
and beautiful in flowers or in fiction.

Then Pindar, and Plato, and Archimedes (who
made enchantments real), and Cicero (who discovered
his tomb), and the Arabs with their architecture, and
the Normans with their gentlemen who were to found
a sovereignty, and the beautiful story of King Robert
and the Angel, and the Sicilian Vespers (horribly so
called), and the true Sicilian Vespers, the gentle " *Ave
Maria*," closing every evening, as it does still, in peace
instead of blood, and ascending from blue seas into
blue heavens out of white-sailed boats.

Item, Bellini, and his Neapolitan neighbour
Paesiello.

Item, the modern Theocritus, not undeservedly so
called; to wit, the Abate Giovanni Meli, possibly of
Grecian stock himself—for his name is the Greek as
well as Sicilian for honey.

Then, every other sort of pastoral poetry, Italian

and English, and Scotch—Tasso, and Guarini, and
Fletcher, and Jonson, and William Brown, and Pope,
and Allan Ramsay.

Item, earthquakes, vines, convents, palm-trees, mul-
berries, pomegranates, aloes, citrons, rocks, gardens,
banditti, pirates, furnaces under the sea, the most
romantic landscapes and vegetation above it, guitars,
lovers, serenades, and the never-to-be-too-often-men-
tioned blue skies and blue waters, whose azure (on the
concentrating Solomon-seal principle) appeared to be
specially represented by our little blue jar.

Lastly, the sweetness, the melancholy, the birth,
the life, the death, the fugitive evil, the constant good,
the threatening Ætna making every moment of life
precious, and the moment of life so precious, and
breathing such a pure atmosphere, as to enable fear
itself to laugh at, nay, to love the threatening Ætna,
and play with it as with a great planetary lion to which
it has become used.

From all this heap of things, or any portion of them,
or anything which they may suggest, we propose, as
from so many different flowers, to furnish our Jar of
Honey, careless whether the flower be sweet or bitter,
provided the result (with the help of his good-will) be
not un-sweet to the reader. For honey itself is not
gathered from sweet flowers only; neither can much of

it be eaten without a qualification of its dulcitude with some plainer food. It can hardly be supposed to be as sweet to the bees themselves, as it is to us. Evil is so made to wait upon good in this world—to quicken it by alarm, to brighten it by contrast, and render it sympathetic by suffering—that although there is quite enough superabundance of it to incite us to its diminution (Nature herself impelling us to do so), yet tears have their delight, as well as laughter; and laughter itself is admonished by tears and pain not to be too excessive. Laughter has occasioned death:—tears have saved more than life. The readers, therefore, will not suppose that we intend (supposing even that we were able) to *cloy* them with sweets. We hope that they will occasionally look very grave over their honey. We should not be disconcerted, if some bright eyes even shed tears over it.

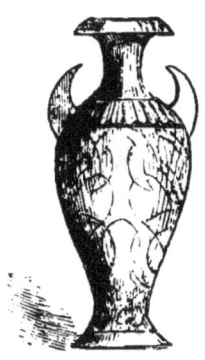

CHAPTER II.

SICILY, AND ITS MYTHOLOGY.

ISLAND OF SICILY, AND MOUNT ÆTNA.—STORIES OF TY-
PHŒUS, POLYPHEMUS, SCYLLA AND CHARYBDIS, GLAUCUS
AND SCYLLA, ALPHEUS AND ARETHUSA, THE SIRENS, AND
THE RAPE OF PROSERPINE.

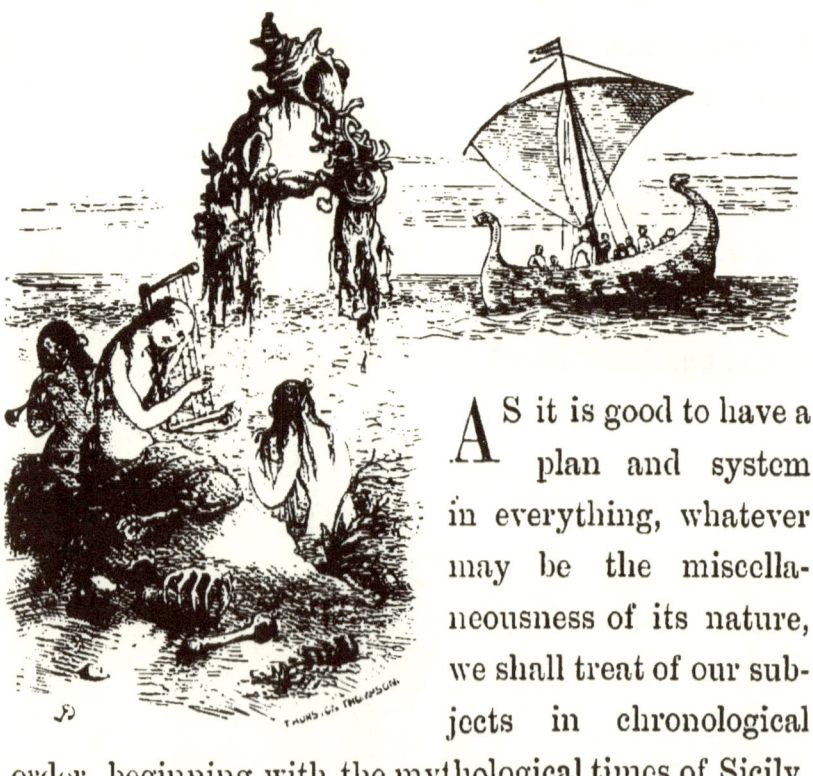

A S it is good to have a plan and system in everything, whatever may be the miscellaneousness of its nature, we shall treat of our subjects in chronological order, beginning with the mythological times of Sicily, and ending with its latest modern poet.

Sicily is an island in the Mediterranean Sea, at the foot of Italy, about half the size of England, and inhabited by a population a fifth less than that of London. Its shape is so regularly three-cornered, that Triangle or Triple-point (Trinacria) was one of its ancient names. Mount Ætna stands on the east, in one of these angles. The coast is very rocky and romantic ; the interior is a combination of rugged mountains and the loveliest plains ; and the soil is so fertile in corn as well as other productions, that Sicily has been called the granary of Europe. The inhabitants are badly governed, and there is great poverty among them ; but movements have taken place of late years that indicate advancement; and the Sicilians, meantime, have all those helps to endurance (perhaps too many) which result from sprightliness of character, united with complexional indolence. They are good-natured but irritable ; have more independence of spirit than their neighbours the Neapolitans ; and are still a pastoral people as of old, making the most of their valleys and their Mount Ætna ; not by activity, but by pipe and song, and superstition.

With this link of their newest and their oldest history we shall begin our Sicilian memories from the beginning.

Did Ætna exist before the human race ? Was it, for ages, a great lonely earth-monster, sitting by the sea

with his rugged woody shoulders and ghastly crown;
now silent and quiet for centuries, like a basking giant;
now roaring to the antediluvian skies; vomiting forth
fire and smoke; drivelling with lava; then silent again
as before; alternately destroying and nourishing the
transitory races of analogous gigantic creatures, mam-
moths, and mastodons, which preceded nobler humanity? Was it produced all at once by some tremendous burst of earth and ocean?—some convulsion, of
which the like has never since been known,—perhaps
with all Sicily hanging at its root: or did it grow, like
other earthly productions, by its own energies and the
accumulations of time? In whatever way it originated,
and however the huge wonder may have behaved itself
at any period, quietly or tremendously, nobody can doubt
that the creature is a benevolent creature,—one of the
securities of the peaceful and profitable existence of the
far greater and more mysterious creature rolling in the
shape of an orb round the sun in midst of its countless
like, and carrying us all along with it in our respective
busy inattentions. We do not presume to inquire how
the necessity for any such evil mode of good arose.
Suffice for us, that the evil itself works to a good purpose;
that the earth, apparently, could not exist without it;
that Nature has adorned it with beauty which is another
good, with fertility which is another, with grandeur

which is another, elevating the mind; and that if human beings prefer risking its neighbourhood with all its occasional calamities, to going and living elsewhere, those calamities are not of its own willing, nor of any unavoidable necessity, nor perhaps will exist always. Suppose Ætna should some day again be left to its solitude, and people resolve to be burnt and buried alive no longer? What a pilgrimage would the mountain be then! What a thought for the poet and the philosopher! What a visit for those who take delight in the borders of fear and terror, and who would love to interrogate Nature the more for the loneliness of her sanctuary!

The first modes of organized life which make their appearance in these remotest ages of Sicily, are of course fabulous modes,—fabulous, but like all fables, symbolical of truth; and what is better than mere truth, of truths poetical. The mythic portion of the history of Sicily is like its region—small, rich, lovely, and terrible. It may be said to consist wholly of the stories of Typhœus, of Polyphemus and the Cyclopes, of Scylla and Charybdis, of the Sirens, of the Rape of Proserpine, of Alpheus and Arethusa, of Acis and Galatea—names, which have become music in the ears of mankind.

What! is Typhœus a musical name? and Polyphemus and the Cyclopes? Yes, of the grander sort organ-like; the bass for the treble of the Sirens; the gloom and terror, along which floats away, through vine and almond, the lovely murmur of Alpheus and Arethusa.

We shall not explain away these beautiful fables into allegory, physics, or any other kind of ungrateful and half-witted prose. They may have had the dullest sources, for aught we know to the contrary, as beautiful streams may have their fountains in the dullest places, or delightful children unaccountably issue from the dullest progenitors; but there they were of old, in Sicily; and here they are among us to this day; in poets' books; in painters' colours; among the delights of every cultivated mind; true as anything else that is known by its effects; spiritual creatures, living and breathing in the enchanted regions of the imagination. The poets took them in hand from infancy, and made them the real and immortal things they are. We shall not deny their analogy with beautiful or grand operations in Nature, as long as the mystery and poetry of those operations are kept in mind. Typhœus, or Typhon, for instance, may, if the etymologist pleases, be the *Tifoon*, or Dreadful Wind, of the Eastern seas; or he may be the *smoking* of Mount Ætna (from τύφω to smoke); or he may comprehend both meanings in one word, derived from some primitive root; for as long as his cause remains a secret, and his effect is poetical, so long the spirit of the mystery may be embodied as imagination pleases. Suffice for us, that the thing is there, somehow. All that we object to in the natural or supernatural historians of such persons, is their stopping at mechanical and prosaical causes, and thinking they settle anything.

This said personage Typhœus is, it must be owned, a tremendous fellow to begin stories with of beautiful Sicily; to put at the head of creations containing so much loveliness. He was a monster of monsters, brought forward by Earth as a last desperate resource in the quarrel of her Giants with the Gods. His stature reached the sky; he had a hundred dragons' heads, vomiting flames; and when it pleased him to express his dissatisfaction, there issued from these heads the roaring and shrieking of a hundred different animals! Jupiter had as hard a task to conquer him as Amadis had with the Endriago.* A good report of the fight is to be found in Hesiod. Heaven trembled, and earth groaned, and ocean flashed with a ghastly radiance, as they lightened and thundered at one another. The king of the gods at length collected all his deity for one tremendous effort, and leaping upon

* See that beautiful book, *Amadis of Gaul*, vol. i. chap. 12, in the admirable translation by Southey.

his antagonist with his whole armoury of thunders, made his foaming mouth hiss in the blaze; the mountain hollows flashed fainter where he lay smitten; the rocks dropped about him like melted lead; and Jupiter tore up the whole island of Sicily, and flung it upon him, by way of detainer for ever. One promontory acted as a presser on one hand; another on another; a third on his legs; and the crater of Mount Ætna was left him for a spiracle. There he lay in the time of Ovid, making the cities tremble as he turned; and there he lies still, for all that Brydone, or Smyth, or even Monsieur Gourbillon has proved to the contrary; though scepticism has attained to such a pitch in that quarter, that the only danger in earthquakes is now attributed to people's not being quick enough with displaying the veil of Saint Agatha.

Compared with this cloud-capped enormity, our old friend Polyphemus (*Many-voice*), the ogre or Fee-Faw-Fum of antiquity, becomes a human being. He and his one-eyed Cyclopes (*Round-eyes*), are the primitive inhabitants of Sicily, before men ploughed and reaped. They kept sheep and goats, and had an eye to business in the cannibal line; though what it was that gave them their name, is not determined; nor is it necessary to trouble the reader with the controversies on that point. Very huge fellows they were, beating Brobdingnagians to nothing. Homer describes Polyphemus as looking like a "woody hill." He kept Ulysses and his companions in his cave to eat them, just as his Oriental counterpart did Sinbad, or as the giants of our childhood proposed to feast on Jack; and when Ulysses put out the eye of roaring *Many-voice* with a firebrand, and got off to sea, the blind monster sent some rocks after the ship, which remain stuck on the coast to this day.

And yet, by the magic of love and sympathy, even Polyphemus has been rendered pathetic. Theocritus made him so with his poetry; and Handel did as much for him in his musical version of the story, especially in those exquisite caressing passages between Acis and Galatea, ("The flocks shall leave the mountains," &c.,) which might fill the most amiable rival with torment. Acis (*Acuteness*) and Galatea (*Milky*)—(we like this fairy-tale restitution of the meanings of ancient names, the example of which was at first set, we believe, by Mr. Keightley)—forgot themselves, however, too far, when they made love before the very eyes of the rival;—not the only instance, we fear, of similar provocation given by the vanity of happy lovers. We regret this ill-breeding the more on account of the monster's hopelessness; and considering the little patience that was to be expected of him, almost pardon the rock which he sent on their ecstatic heads.

Gay's verses on this occasion would not have been unworthy of Theocritus :—

ACIS AND GALATEA.   [*Duet.*]

The flocks shall leave the mountains,
    The woods the turtle-dove,
The nymphs forsake the fountains,
    Ere I forsake my love.

POLYPHEMUS.   [*Solo.*]

Torture! fury! rage! despair!
I cannot, cannot, cannot bear.

ACIS AND GALATEA.

Not showers to larks so pleasing,
    Nor sunshine to the bee ;
Not sleep to toil so easing,
    As those dear smiles to me.

POLYPHEMUS HURLS THE ROCK.

Fly swift, thou massy ruin, fly :
Die, presumptuous Acis, die.

Scylla and Charybdis, or Scylla and Glaucus rather, is a far more appalling story of jealousy. Scylla properly belongs to the opposite coast of Naples; but as she and her fellow-monster Charybdis are usually named together, and the latter tenanted the Sicilian coast, and the strait between them was very narrow, she is not to be omitted in Sicilian fable. Charybdis (quasi Chalybdis, *Hiding ?* though some derive it from two words signifying to "gape" and "absorb") was a personage of a very unique sort, to wit, a female freebooter; who, having stolen the oxen of Hercules, was condemned to be a whirlpool, and suck ships into its gulf. Nevertheless she was a horror not to be compared with Scylla, though the latter was thought less dangerous. Mr. Keightley has so well told this story out of Homer, that we must repeat it in his words :—

"Having escaped the Sirens, and shunned the Wandering Rocks, which Circe told him lay beyond the mead of these songsters, Odysseus (Ulysses) came to the terrific Scylla and Charybdis, between which the goddess had informed him his course lay. She said he would come to two lofty cliffs opposite each other, between which he must pass. One of these cliffs towers to such a height, that its summit is for ever enveloped in clouds ; and no man, even if he had twenty hands and as many feet, could ascend it. In the middle of this cliff, she says, is a cave facing the west, but so high, that a man in a ship passing under it could not shoot up to it with a bow. In this den dwells Scylla (*Bitch*), whose voice sounds like that of a young whelp : she had twelve feet *and six long necks, with a terrific head, and three rows of close-set teeth on each*. Evermore she *stretches out these necks* and catches the porpoises, sea-dogs, and other large animals of the sea,

which swim by, and out of every ship that passes *each
month takes a man.*

"The opposite rock, the goddess informs him, is
much lower, for a man could shoot over it. A wild fig-
tree grows on it, stretching his branches down to the
water: but beneath, 'divine Charybdis' three times each
day absorbs and regorges the dark water. It is much
more dangerous, she adds, to pass Charybdis than Scylla.

"As Odysseus sailed by, Scylla took *six of his crew*;
and when, after he had lost his ship and companions,
he was carried by wind and wave, as he floated on a
part of the wreck, between the monsters, the mast by
which he supported himself was sucked in by Charybdis. He held by the fig-tree, till it was thrown out
again, and resumed his voyage."—*Mythology of Ancient
Greece and Italy.* See. edit., p. 271.

It has been thought by some, that by the word
Scylla is meant the bitch of the sea-dog, or seal—a
creature often found on this coast. Be this as it may
(and the seal having a more human look than the dog,
might suggest a more frightful image, to say nothing of
its being more appropriate to the water), who was
Scylla ? and how came she to be this tremendous
monster ? From the jealousy of Circe. Scylla was
originally a beautiful maiden, fond of the company of
the sea-nymphs ; and Glaucus (*Sea-green*), a god of

the sea, was in love with her. She did not like him; and Glaucus applied to Circe for help, from her skill in magic. Circe fell in love with the lover, and being enraged with the attractions that made him refuse her, poisoned the water in which Scylla bathed. The result was the conversion of the beauty's lower limbs into a set of barking dogs. The dogs became part of her; and when in her horror she thought to drive them back, she found herself " hauling " them along—one creature, says Ovid, hauling many :

Quos fugit, attrahit una.—*Metam.* xiv. v. 63.

This is very dreadful. Yet Homer's creature is more so. Scylla's proceedings, in the *Odyssey*, exactly resemble the accounts which mariners have given of a huge sea-polypus—a cousin of the kraken, or sea-serpent—who thrusts its gigantic feelers over the deck of an unsuspecting ship, and carries off seamen. There is a picture of it in one of the editions of Buffon. But the dog-like barking, and the terrific head and teeth, to which the imagination gives something of a human aspect, leave the advantage of the horrible still on the side of the poet.

An old English poet, Lodge, at a time when our earliest dramatists, who were university men, had set the example of a love of classical fable, wrote a poem

on *Glaucus and Scylla,* in which there are passages of
the loveliest beauty; though it was spoilt, as a whole,
with conceits. In describing the nymph's yellow hair,
he makes use of a Sicilian image, very fit for our Blue
Jar :—

> Her hair, not truss'd, but scatter'd on her brow,
> Surpassing Hybla's honey.

We are to suppose it lying in sunny flakes. Lodge,
though he was an Oxford man, or perhaps for that
reason, has curiously mixed up Paganism and Christianity in Glaucus's complaint of his mistress : but the
second verse is fine, and the last truly lover-like and
touching :—

> Alas, sweet nymphs, my godhead's all in vain ;
> For why? *this breast includes immortal pain.*

> Scylla hath eyes, but two sweet eyes hath Scylla ;
> Scylla hath hands, fair hands, but coy in touching :
> Scylla in wit surpasseth grave Sibylla :

(This is the Sibyl of Æneas)

> Scylla hath words, but words well-stored with grutching ;
> Scylla, a saint in look, no saint in scorning,
> *Look saint-like, Scylla, lest I die with mourning.*

The modulation and antithetical turn of these verses
will remind the reader not only of Lodge's friends, Peele
and Greene, who had both a fine ear for music, but of
Shakspeare's first production, *Venus and Adonis,* in
which he exhibited that fondness for classical fable

which never forsook him. It is remarkable indeed, that the old English poets, and those true successors of theirs whom we have seen in our own time, have been almost more Greek in this respect than the Greeks themselves. Spenser was half made up of it; Milton could not help introducing it in *Paradise Lost;* and it was rescued from the degradation it underwent in the French school of poetry, with its cant about the " Paphian bower," and its identifications of Venus and Chloe, by the inspired Muse of Keats. The young English poet has told the present story in his *Endymion*, though not in his best manner, except where he speaks of Circe; of the inflictions of whose sorcery he gives a scene of the finest and most appalling description :—

> *A sight too fearful for the feel of fear.—*
> In thicket hid—

(It is Glaucus who is speaking, and whom the poet represents as having been beguiled into Circe's love)—

> In thicket hid I curs'd *the haggard scene—*
> The banquet of my arms, my arbour queen,
> Seated upon an uptorn forest root,
> And all around her shapes, wizard and brute,
> *Laughing and wailing*, grovelling, serpenting.
> *Fierce, wan,*
> *And tyrannizing was the lady's look*,
> As over them a gnarled staff she shook.

The look of a sorceress, full of bad passions, was never painted more strongly than in the meeting of those

epithets, "wan and tyrannizing;" and the word
"lady" makes the fierceness more shocking.

But Keats had not the heart to make the love-part
of the story end unhappily, much less to endure the
brutification of the lovely limbs of Scylla. He revived
her to be put into a Lovers' Elysium. So, in telling
the story of Alpheus and Arethusa, he will not let
Arethusa reject Alpheus willingly. He makes her
lament the necessity as one of the train of Diana; and
leaves us to conclude that the lovers became happy.
It would hardly be necessary to tell any reader (only
it is as pleasant to repeat these stories, as it is to
hear beautiful old airs) that Alpheus was a river-god
of Greece, who fell in love with the wood-nymph
Arethuse; and that the latter, praying for help to
Diana, was converted into a stream, and pursued under
land and *sea* by the other enamoured water, as far as
the island of Sicily, where the streams became united.
The strangeness of the adventure, and the beauty of the
names, have made everybody in love with the story.
All the world knows how "divine Alpheus," as Milton
says—

> Stole under seas to meet his Arethuse ;

or rather they all knew the *fact ;* but the *how,* or
manner of it, was a puzzle, till Keats related the
adventure as it was witnessed by Endymion in a

grotto under the sea. The lover of the Moon suddenly
heard strange distant echoes, which seemed—

> The ghosts, the dying swells
> Of noises far away—hist!—Hereupon
> He kept an anxious ear. The humming tone
> Came louder; and behold! there, as he lay,
> On either side out-gush'd, with misty spray,
> A copious spring; and both together dash'd
> Swift, mad, fantastic round the rocks, and lash'd
> Among the conchs and shells of the lofty grot,
> Leaving a trickling dew.

(These are the two living streams, one in pursuit of
the other.)

> At last they shot
> Down from the ceiling's height, pouring a noise
> As of some breathless racers, whose hopes poise
> Upon the last few steps, and with spent force
> Along the ground they took a winding course.
> Endymion follow'd, for it seem'd that one
> Ever pursued, the other strove to shun.

After a while, he hears a whispering dialogue, in
which the female voice shows plainly enough, that the
speaker would stay if she might; but suddenly the
severe face of Diana is before her, and in an instant

> Fell
> Those two sad streams adown a fearful dell;

and Endymion puts up a prayer for their escape.

When the writer of the present book was in Italy,
he saw on a mantelpiece a card inscribed, *Le Marquis
de Retuse.* This was the Frenchified denomination of

4

a Sicilian nobleman, who, strangely combining Greek
and Gothic in his title, was no less a personage than
the *Marquis of Arethusa!* He was proprietor of the
spot where the fountain exists under its old name,
though, according to travellers, deplorably altered; for
it has become, says one of them, the public "wash-
tub!" It is the Syracusan laundry. Divers, he
informs us, are the jokes cracked on the "nymphs"
that now attend it. Some critics are of opinion, that
such were the "only nymphs" that ever existed; and
they are very merry over the fallen condition of the
once exquisite Arethusa. Poor devils! taking pains to
vulgarize their perceptions, and diminish the amount
of grace and joy. As if Arethusa, like themselves, were
at the mercy of a homely association; or all that had
been written about her was no better than their own
account with the laundress! They flatter themselves.
They leave her just where she was—everywhere, and
immortal. It may not be very pleasant to look for a
poetic fountain, and find a laundry; but the imagination
is a poor one indeed, which is to be overwhelmed by
it. The nymphs of minds like these could never have
been very different from laundresses, if the truth were
known; or, at the utmost, of little higher stock than
such as laundresses and milliners are the making of.

There are two things, we confess, about the *Sirens*,

that perplex us. In the first place, we never found anything particularly attractive in the songs attributed to them, not even by Homer; and secondly, we are too much in the secret of their deformity. We know that they were ghastly monsters, bird-harpies with women's heads, and surrounded with human bones; and the consequence is, we can never find them in the least degree enticing. It is to no purpose that they combine stringed with wind instruments, and a voice crowning all. One of them may call herself *Fair-Goddess* (Leucothea), and another *Fine-voice* (Ligeia), and the third *Maiden-face* (Parthenope). We know all about them, and are not to be taken in. It would require a dream as horrible as Coleridge's *Pains of Sleep* to bring our antipathy into any communication with them —to make us walk in our sleep towards their quarter:—

> Desire with loathing strangely mix'd,
> On wild and hateful objects fix'd ;
> Fantastic passions, maddening brawl,
> And shame and terror over all.

When the modern poets turned the Sirens into mermaids, they vastly improved the breed. A woman, we grant, who is half a fish, is not a desideratum ; but she is better than a great human-faced bird hopping about ; and besides, the conformation of the creatures being thus altered, we are not so sure they will do us harm, especially as the poets treat them with com-

parative respect, sometimes even with tenderness.
The names above mentioned acquire a double elegance
in the adjurations of the Spirit in *Comus* :—

> By Thetis' tinsel-slipper'd feet,
> And the songs of Sirens sweet,
> By dead Parthenope's dear tomb,
> And fair Ligeia's golden comb,
> Wherewith she sits on diamond rocks,
> *Sleeking her soft alluring locks.*

These alluring locks come home to us. We have seen
such at our elbows, and can hear the comb passing
through them.

Spenser increased the number of the Sirens to five,
and expressly designated them as mermaids :—

> And now they nigh approached to the stead
> Whereas those mermaids dwelt. It was a still
> *And calmy bay*, on th' one side sheltered
> *With the broad shadow of an hoary hill ;*
> On th' other side an high rock towered still,
> That 'twixt them both a pleasant port they made,
> And did like an half theatre fulfil.
> There those five sisters had continual trade,
> *And used to bathe themselves in that deceiptful shade.*
> —*Fairy Queen*, book ii. canto 12.

This line is so soft and gently drawn out, and the
place so sweet and natural, that when Sirens like these
begin to sing, we really feel in danger. We do not
wonder that the poet's hero desired his boatman to

> Row easily,
> And let him hear some part of their rare melody.

WE have kept the most beautiful of the Sicilian mythic stories to conclude with : for such, doubtless, is the *Rape of Proserpine*. It is full of the most striking contrasts of grandeur and beauty. Both heaven and hell are in it—the freshest vernal airs, with the depths of Tartarus ; and the hearts of a mother and daughter beat through all. It is a tale at once of the wildest preternaturalism and the most familiar domestic tenderness. The daughter of Ceres is gathering flowers, with other damsels of her own age, in the Vale of Enna, intent upon nothing but seeing who shall get

the finest. Suddenly, in the midst of the violets and
jonquils, there is an earthquake : a noise is heard like
the coming of a thousand chariots ; the earth bursts
open ; and a rapid, majestic figure appears, like a
swarthy Jupiter, who, sweeping by Proserpine, whirls
her away with him into his car, and prepares to rush
down through another opening. Of all her attendants,
the nymph Cyane alone has the courage to bid him
stop, and ask him why he dares take away the
daughter of Ceres. He makes no answer, but, knit-
ting his brows like thunderbolts, smites the fountain
over which she presided with his iron mace, and
dashes down through it with his prey. It is the
King of Hell himself, tired of celibacy, and resolved
to have the fairest creature on earth for his wife.

The cries of Proserpine become fainter as the earth
closes over them ; but they have been heard by Ceres
herself, who comes, with all the speed of a divine
being, to see what is the matter. She can discern
nothing ; the tranquillity of the scene is restored ;
Cyane has melted away in tears. The goddess seeks
everywhere in vain. She travels by day and by night,
lit by two flaming pines from Mount Ætna. At length
she learns who has got her child ; and, by the intervention of Jupiter, Proserpine is allowed to come to
earth and see her. The mother and daughter are half

drowned in tears, half absorbed in delight, and Jupiter would prevent their separation, but is not able; for Proserpine has eaten of a fatal fruit, compulsory of her continuance with Pluto; and all that can be done, is to stipulate for her being half a year with her mother, on condition of her being a good wife during the other half. Ceres makes a virtue of the necessity, seeing that her daughter is married to the brother of Jove; and Proserpine is content to divide the throne of Tartarus, and walk in gardens of her own, splendid, though subterraneous.

The ancient poets made these gardens consist of all the flowers which she had been accustomed to gather in Sicily; but modern imagination, which (with leave be it said) is still finer than theirs, and sees beauty beyond its ordinary manifestation in the fitness of things, and in the balance of good and evil, has told us, through the inspired medium of Spenser, that the garden was such a garden as might have been expected from "the grandeur of the glooms" in those lower regions:—

> There mournful cypress grew in greatest store,
> And trees of bitter gall, and ebon sad,
> Deep-sleeping poppy, and black hellebore,
> Cold coloquintida, and tetra *mad*,
> Mortal samnitis, and cicuta bad,
> With which the unjust Athenians made to die
> Wise Socrates, who thereof quaffing glad

Pour'd out his life and last philosophy
To the fair Critias, his dearest belamy.
The Garden of Prosèrpina this hight ;
And in the midst thereof *a silver seat*,
With a thick arbour goodly overdight,
In which she often used from open heat
Herself to shroud, and pleasures to entreat ;
Next thereunto did grow a goodly tree,
With branches broad dispread, and body great,
Clothed with leaves, that none the fruit might see,
And loaden all with fruit as thick as it might be.

Their fruit were golden apples, glistering bright.
—*Fairy Queen*, book ii. canto 7.

Here we see, that Proserpine enjoyed herself in the
lower regions, though among flowers of a different kind
from those to which she had been accustomed. She
became used to the place, and found pleasures even in
Tartarus. And reasonably. First, because she needed
them ; and in the second place, because she knew there
was good as well as evil there, and that the evil itself
contained good. The hemlock was "bad," inasmuch as
it killed Socrates, but it was good, also, for many a
medicinal cup. "Deep-sleeping poppy" was a very
kindly fellow, if properly treated ; and all the flowers,
after their kind, were full of beauty. Flowers cannot
help being beautiful. Then there was the Silver Seat
and the Golden Tree ; and it is manifest, that the

summer sun used to come there through some unknown ravine, to say nothing of Wordsworth's

Calm pleasures and majestic pains.

We do not, to be sure, see what good Tantalus's eternal thirst could have been to him, or the everlasting wheel to Ixion; but, probably, on coming up to those gentlemen, we should have found they were visions, put there to make us " snatch a fearful joy " at thinking we were not among them in *propriâ personâ*.

And so we take leave of the beautiful ancient fables of Sicily, having found honey for our Jar even in the fields of Pluto.

CHAPTER III.

GLANCES AT ANCIENT SICILIAN HISTORY AND BIOGRAPHY.

VICISSITUDES OF SICILIAN GOVERNMENT.—GLANCES AT
PHALARIS, STESICHORUS, EMPEDOCLES, HIERO I., SIMO-
NIDES, EPICHARMUS, DIONYSIUS I., DAMON AND PYTHIAS,
DAMOCLES, DIONYSIUS II., DION, PLATO, AGATHOCLES,
HANNIBAL, HIERO II., THEOCRITUS, ARCHIMEDES, MARCEL-
LUS, VERRES ; AND PARTICULARS RELATING TO GELLIAS.

ICILY being
one of those
small, beauti-
ful, and abun-
dant countries
which excite
the cupidity of
larger ones, has
had as many
foreign masters
as the poor
Princess of Ba-
bylon in Boc-

caccio, who, on her way to be married to the King of Colchos, fell into the hands of nine husbands. First, in all probability, came subjugators from the Italian continent ; then Phœnicians, or commercial invaders; then, undoubtedly, Greeks; then Carthaginians ; then Romans, Goths, Saracens, Normans, Germans, Frenchmen, Spaniards, Gallo-Spaniards, Frenchmen again, Gallo-Spaniards again ; and in the possession of these last it remains. Under the Greeks, its cities grew into powerful independent states. Syracuse was once twenty-two miles in circumference. The most prominent names in the ancient history of Sicily are touched upon in the following list.

Phalaris, tyrant of Agrigentum, who roasted people in a brazen bull, in which he was ultimately made to roar himself. That is to say, if the bull be true. For the reign of this prince was at so remote a period, and the excitement of exaggeration is so tempting, that the sight of the bull in after times proves no more than was proved by the brazen wolf of Romulus and Remus. The age of Phalaris was that of the Prophet Daniel.

Stesichorus, a majestic lyrical poet, in one of whose fragments is to be found the beautiful fiction of the Golden Boat of the Sun. The Sun-God sails in it, invisibly, round the Northern Sea in the night-time, so as to be ready to re-appear in the East in the morning.

Empedocles, the Pythagorean philosopher. He is accused of leaping into Ætna, in the hope of being supernaturally missed, and so taken for a god—a project betrayed by the ejection of one of his brazen sandals. But a philosopher may perish by a volcano, as Pliny did, without giving envy a right to make him a laughing-stock.

Hiero the First, of Syracuse ; a bad prince, but a possessor of good horses and charioteers ; for whose victories in the Olympic games his name has become celebrated by means of Pindar. Hiero is the great name in the Racing Calendar of antiquity.

Simonides, the elegiac poet. He was a native of Ceos, but lived much, and died in Sicily, where he was a great favourite. His repeated delays and final answer to Hiero, when desired to give a definition of the Deity, have been deservedly celebrated, and are a lesson to presumption for all time. He first requested a day to consider ; then two more days ; then doubled and redoubled the number ; till the king, demanding the reason of this conduct, was told by the poet that " the longer he considered the question, the more impossible he found it to answer."

Epicharmus, the supposed founder of comedy. He

was a great philosopher as well as poet, and furnished
no little matter to Plato. He died at ninety, some say
at ninety-seven, a longevity attributable to the modera-
tion of his way of life, and the serenity of his temper.
He says in one of his fragments :—

> A darling and a grace is Peace of Mind ;
> She lives next door to Temperance.

Dionysius, tyrant of Syracuse (the Elder).   He
wrote bad verses; slept in a bed with a trench round it
and a drawbridge; and, for fear of a barber, burnt
away his beard with hot walnut-shells. What a razor!
Dionysius had abilities enough to become the more
hateful for his capricious and detestable qualities.
Probably he had a spice of madness in him, which
power exasperated.   Ariosto has turned him to fine
account in his personification of Suspicion.

Damon and Pythias, the famous friends.   One of
them became surety to Dionysius for the other's
appearance at the scaffold, and was not disappointed.
Dionysius begged to be admitted a third in the part-
nership!—the most ridiculous thing, perhaps, that even
the tyrant ever did.

Damocles, the courtly gentleman, who pronounced
Dionysius the happiest man on earth. He was treated
by his master to a " proof of the pudding " which
tyrants eat.   He sat crowned at the head of a luxu-

rious banquet, in the midst of odours, music, and homage ; and saw, suspended by a hair over his head, a naked sword. This, it must be confessed, was a happy thought of the royal poet—a practical epigram of the very finest point.

Dionysius, tyrant of Syracuse (the Younger), who, on his ejection from the throne, is said to have become a schoolmaster at Corinth ; " in order," says Cicero, " that he might still be a scourger somehow."

Dion, his relation, and Timoleon of Corinth, the great but unhappy fratricide ; both of whom advanced the liberties of Syracuse.

Plato ; who visited both the Dionysiuses, to induce them to become philosophers ! He might as well have asked tigers in a sheepfold to prefer a dish of green pease.

Agathocles the Potter, tyrant of the whole island ; who piqued himself on outdoing the cruelties of Phalaris. His objection to the brazen bull was, that you could not see the face of the person tortured ; so he invented a hollow iron man with an open visor, in order that he might contemplate the face of the occupant, while heating over a slow fire. But let us hope the story is not true ; for, though things as horrible have taken place in the world, the wicked themselves have been calumniated.

Hannibal, during the Punic wars. You see him, at this period of time, looming in the distance over every other object, and standing in Sicily like a great visiting giant. He is accounted, we believe, on military authority, the greatest captain that ever lived. So different is success in art from prosperity in fortune.

Hiero the Second, of Syracuse. A prudent and popular ally of the Romans. He showed no great favour to Theocritus. He built a huge toy-ship, in which were gardens, a wrestling-ground, rooms full of pictures and statues, floors with subjects from Homer painted in mosaic, and eight fortified towers! We should like to know what Tom Bowling would have said to it. When it was completed, it was found that there was no harbour in Sicily fit to receive it; so the king sent it as a present to Ptolemy Philadelphus of Egypt.

Theocritus, the great pastoral and miscellaneous poet, for pastoral was not his only, or his highest excellence. Circumstances appear to have made a present of *him* also, as well as the ship, to King Ptolemy; for Hiero neglected, and Philadelphus patronised him.

Archimedes, kinsman of Hiero. His wonderful mechanical inventions are among the daily instruments of utility all over the world. The Romans were obliged to suspend their operations against Syracuse, solely by the terror he occasioned them with his cranes that lifted

their ships, and his glasses that burnt them. When
the city was taken, orders were given to spare the great
man, and bring him before the Roman general, that he
might be duly honoured; but a stupid soldier unwit-
tingly despatched him, provoked at having been requested to wait while the philosopher finished a problem.
The problem part of the story is not very likely. Sir
Isaac Newton carried abstraction far enough, when he
forgot that he had eaten his dinner, or when he used a
lady's finger for a tobacco-stopper; but an engineer for-
getting his own city while it was being taken by storm
and howling about his ears, seems a little too hard a
sample of it.

Marcellus, the Roman general on this occasion. His
eyes are said to have filled with tears at the thought of
all that was going to happen to the conquered city. He
was the first successful opposer of Hannibal. When
reproached for carrying off paintings and other works
of art from Sicily, he said he did it to refine the minds
of his countrymen. His tears render every anecdote
of him precious to posterity.

Verres, one of the governors of Sicily while it was
a Roman province;—infamous for the tyranny and
effrontery of his extortions, even if but half of what
Cicero said of him was true : for we must confess that
we seldom believe more of what is told us by that

illustrious talker; especially as he warns us against
himself, by contradicting in one passage what he says
in another. *Vide* his recommendations of people in his
letters, and his discommendations of them in other
letters, privately sent at the same time. Also, his
vituperations and panegyrics of the same individuals
concerned in the civil wars, just as it suited him to con-
demn or to court them; to say nothing of his divorces
and weddings for interest's sake. We have said the more
of him in this place because he too, at one time, held
the office of governor in Sicily, where he discovered the
tomb of Archimedes—a memorial, alas! forgotten by
the philosopher's countrymen in less than a century
and a half after his death! They wanted to "stand
out" Cicero, that there was no such thing. However,
they had not forgotten Theocritus. The greatest mechanical movers of the earth affect the imagination less
than they ought to do, and the heart not at all. The
lever and the screw, as the steam-engine will, become
homely commonplaces; whereas love and song, and
the beauties of Nature, are sought with transport, like
holidays after business.

The names thus enumerated (for little or no interest
attends the Goth and Vandal portion of the history of
this island), may be said to point to all the characters
of any importance in Sicilian antiquity, one only ex-

cepted.   This individual we have kept to the last,
though he was little more than a private person, and
is not at all famous.   But we have a special regard for
him; far more indeed, than for most of those who have
been mentioned ; and we think that such of our readers
as are not already acquainted with him, will have one
too; for he was of that tip-top class of human beings
called *Good Fellows*, and a very prince of the race.
What renders him a still better fellow than he might
otherwise have been, and doubles his heroical qualities
in discerning eyes, is, that he was but an insignificant
little body to look at, and not very well shaped ;—a
mannikin, in short, that Sir Godfrey Kneller's nephew,
the slave-trader, who rated the painter and his friend
Pope at less than " ten guineas' " worth " the pair,"
would probably not have valued at more than two
pounds five.

The name of this great unknown was Gellias, and
you must search into by-corners, even of Sicilian
history, to find anything about him; but he was just
the man for our Jar;—sweet as the honey that Samson
found in the jaws of the lion.

Gellias was the richest man in the rich city of
Agrigentum.   The Agrigentines, according to a saying
of their countryman Empedocles, were famous for
" building as if they were to live for ever, and feasting

as if they were to die next day." But they were as
good-natured and hospitable as they were festive; and
Gellias, in accordance with the superiority of his circumstances, was the most good-natured and hospitable of
them all. His magnificence resembled that of a Barme-
cide. Slaves were stationed at the gates of his noble
mansion to invite strangers to enter. His cellar had
three hundred reservoirs cut in the solid rock, each containing seven hundred gallons of wine at their service.
One day five hundred horsemen halted at his door, who
had been overtaken by a storm. He lodged and entertained them all; and, by way of dry clothes, made each
man a present of a new tunic and robe.

His wit appears to have been as ready as it was
pungent. He was sent ambassador on some occasion
to the people of Centauripa, a place at the foot of
Mount Ætna. When he rose in the assembly to
address them, his poor little figure made so ridiculous
a contrast with his mission, that they burst into fits
of laughter. Gellias waited his time, and then requested them not to be astonished;—"for," said he, "it
is the custom with Agrigentum to suit the ambassador
to his locality; to send noble-looking persons to great
cities, and insignificant ones to the insignificant."

The combined magnanimity and address of this
sarcasm are not to be surpassed. Ambassadors are

privileged people; but they have not always been spared
by irritated multitudes; yet our hero did not hesitate to
turn the ridicule of the Centauripans on themselves.
He "showed up" the smallness of their pretensions,
both as a community and as observers. He did not
blink the fact of his own bodily insignificance—too sore
a point with little people in general, notwithstanding
the fact that many of the greatest spirits of the world
have resided in frames as petty. He made it the very
ground for exposing the still smaller pretensions of the
souls and understandings of his deriders. Or, supposing
that he said it with a good-humoured smile,—with an
air of rebuke to their better sense,—still the address
was as great, and the magnanimity as candid. He not
only took the "bull by the horns," but turned it with
his mighty little hands into a weapon of triumph. Such
a man, insignificant as his general exterior may have
been, must, after all, have had something fine in some
part of it—something great in some part of its expression; probably fine eyes, and a smile full of benignity.

Gellias proved that his soul was of the noblest order,
not only by a princely life, but by the heroical nature of
his death. Agrigentum lay on the coast opposite Car-
thage. It had been a flourishing place, partly by reason
of its commerce with that city; but was at last insulted
by it and subdued. Most of the inhabitants fled.

Among those who remained was Gellias. He fancied that his great wealth, and his renown for hospitality, would procure him decent treatment. Finding, however, that the least to be expected of the enemy was captivity, he set fire to a temple into which he had conveyed his wealth, and perished with it in the flames; thus, says Stolberg, at once preventing "the profanation of the place, the enriching of the foe, and the disgrace of slavery."

There ought to be a book devoted to the history of those whose reputations have not received their due. It would make a curious volume. It would be old in the materials, novel in the interest, and of equal delight and use. It is a startling reflection, that while men, such as this Gellias, must be dug up from the by-ways of history, its high-road is three-parts full of people who would never have been heard of, but for accidents of time and place. Take, for instance, the majority of the Roman emperors, of those of Germany, of the turbulent old French noblesse, and indeed of three-fourths, perhaps nine-tenths, of historical names all over the world. The reflection, nevertheless, suggests one of a more consolatory kind, namely, that genius and great qualities are not the only things to be considered in this world;—that commonplace also has its right to be heard; common affections and common wants;—ay,

the more in the latter case, because they are common.
The worst of it is, that commonplace in power is not
fond of allowing this right to its brother commonplace
out of it.   The progress of knowledge, however, tends
to a greater impartiality; and the consideration of this
fact must be the honey, meantime, to many a bitter
thought.

CHAPTER IV.

THEOCRITUS.

PASTORAL POETRY.—SPECIMENS OF THE STRENGTH AND
COMIC HUMOUR OF THEOCRITUS—THE PRIZE-FIGHT BE-
TWEEN POLLUX AND AMYCUS—THE SYRACUSAN GOSSIPS.

PASTORAL poetry is supposed to have originated in Sicily, at one and the same time with comedy. At all events, it was perfected there. Comedy is understood to have been suggested by the licence with which it was the custom for peasants to rail at passengers, and at one another, during the jollity of the vintage; and pastoral poetry was at first nothing but the more rustical part of comedy. Its great master, Theocritus, arose during a period of refinement; and being a man of a universal genius, with a particular regard for the country, perfected this homelier kind of pastoral, and at the same time anticipated all the others. His single scenes are the germ of the pastoral drama. He is as clownish as Gay, as domestic as Allan Ramsay, as elegant as Virgil and Tasso, and (with the allowance for the difference between ancient and modern imagination) as poetical as Fletcher; and in passion he beats them all. In no other pastoral poetry is there anything to equal his *Polyphemus*.

The world has long been sensible of this superiority. But, in one respect, even the world has not yet done justice to Theocritus. The world, indeed, takes a long time, or must have a twofold blow given it as manifest and sustained as Shakspeare's to entertain two ideas at once respecting anybody. It has been said of wit, that it indisposes people to admit a serious claim on the part of its possessor; and pastoral poetry subjects a man to the like injustice, by reason of its humble modes of life, and its gentle scenery. People suppose that he can handle nothing stronger than a crook. They should read Theocritus's account of Hercules slaying the lion, or of the " stand-up fight," the regular and tremendous " set-to," between Pollux and Amycus. The best

Moulsey-Hurst business was a feather to it. Theocritus was a son of Ætna—all peace and luxuriance in ordinary, all fire and wasting fury when he chose it. He was a genius equally potent and universal; and it is a thousand pities that unknown circumstances in his life hindered him from completing the gigantic fragments, which seem to have been portions of some intended great work on the deeds of Hercules, perhaps on the Argonautic Expedition. He has given us Hercules and the Serpents, Hercules and Hylas, Hercules and the Lion, and the pugilistical contest of the demigod's kinsman with a barbarian ; and the epithalamium of their relation Helen may have been designed as a portion of the same multifarious poem—an anticipation of the romance of modern times, and of the glory of Ariosto. What a loss ! *

* There have been writers who concluded that Theocritus did not write some of these poems, *because* the style of them differed from that of his pastorals. "As though " (says Mr. Chapman, his best translator) "the same poet could not possibly excel in different styles." But this is the way the opinions we have alluded to come up. A writer's powers are turned against himself, and his very property is to be denied him, because critics of this kind have brains for nothing but one species of handicraft. It is lucky for the human being in the abstract, that he is gifted with tears and smiles ; otherwise one or the other of those natural possessions would assuredly have been called in question. In fact, the marvel is, not that genius should deal in both, but that it should ever show itself incapable of either. Exclusive gravity and exclusive levity are alike a solecism, as far as regards the common source of emotion, which is sensitiveness to impressions.

In the poem on the *Prize-fight* (for such is really the subject, the prize being the vanquished man), Pollux, the demigod, one of the sons of Leda by Jupiter, goes to shore from the ship Argo, with his brother Castor, to get some water. They arrive at a beautiful fountain in a wood, by the side of which is sitting a huge overbearing-looking fellow (ἀνὴρ ὑπέροπλος, man presuming on his strength), who returns their salutation with insolence. The following, without any great violence to the letter of the ancient dialogue, may be taken as a sample of its spirit. The ruffian is addressed by Pollux :—

THE PRIZE-FIGHT BETWEEN POLLUX AND AMYCUS.

POLLUX. Good day, friend. What sort of people, pray, live hereabouts?

RUFFIAN. I see no good day when I see strangers.

P. Don't be disturbed. We are honest people who ask the question, and come of an honest stock.

R. I'm not disturbed at all, and don't require to learn it from such as you.

P. You're an ill-mannered, insolent clown.

R. I'm such as you see me. I never came meddling with you in your country.

P. (*good-humouredly.*) Come and meddle, and we'll help you to a little hospitality to take home with you.

R. Keep it to yourselves : I neither give nor take.

P. (*smiling.*) Well, my good friend, may we have a taste of your spring?

R. Ask your throats when they're dry.

P. Come, what's your demand for it? What are we to pay?

R. Hands up, and man against man.

P. What, a fight; or is it to be a kicking-match?

R. A fight; and I would advise you to look about you.

P. I do, and can't even see my antagonist.

R. Here he sits. You'll find me no woman, I can tell you.

P. Good; and what are we to fight for? What's the prize?

R. Submission. If you win, I'm to be at your service; and if I win, you're to be at mine.

P. Why, those are the terms of cocks upon dunghills.

R. Cocks or lions, those are my terms, and you'll have the water on no other.

With these words, Amycus (for it was he—a son of Neptune—and the greatest pugilist but one, then known in the world) blew a blast on a shell, and a multitude of long-haired Bebrycians (his countrymen) came pouring in about the plane-tree, under which he had been sitting. Castor went and called his brother shipmates out of the Argo, and the combatants, putting on their gauntlets, faced one another, and set to.

ROUND THE FIRST.

The contest began by trying to see which of the two should get the sun in his rear. Pollux obtained this advantage over the big man by dint of his wit (for though a demigod himself, he was less in bulk). The

giant, finding the sun full on his face, pushed forward
in a rage; and striking out further than he intended,
laid himself open to a blow on the chin. This enraged
him the more; and pushing still forward, he hung in a
manner over his enemy, thinking with his huge body to
bear him down. His people encouraged the project
with a great shout; and the Argonauts, not to be
behindhand, gave their champion another; for, in
truth, they were not without apprehensions as to the
result, seeing how enormous the body was. But the
son of Jove slipped hither and thither, lacerating him
all the while with double quick blows, and thus re-
pulsing the endeavour. Amycus was compelled fairly
to hold himself up as well as he could, for he was
drunk with blows, and so he stood, vomiting blood.
The noise of voices arose on all sides from the spectators, for his face was a mass of ulcers; and it was so
swollen that you could hardly see his eyes. The son of
Jove kept him still in a state of confusion, forcing him
to waste his strength and spirits by striking out hither
and thither to no purpose. At last, on seeing him
about to lose his senses, he planted a final blow on the
top of his nose, betwixt the eyebrows, and the giant
fell at his length on the grass, with his face upwards.

ROUND THE SECOND.

Amycus rose on recovering his senses, and the fight was renewed with double fury. The dull-witted giant thought to knock the life out of his antagonist speedily, by striking heavily at his chest; but, by this proceeding, he again laid his face open, and the invincible Pollux disfigured and made it a heap of filth with unseemly blows. The flesh, which had before been so puffed up, now seemed to subside and melt away; the whole huge creature seemed to become little, while the less one assumed a greater aspect, and looked fresher for his toil.

"Say, Muse, for thou knowest," how it was that the son of Jove finally overcame " the *gluttonous* " * giant.

" Thinking to do something great, the big Bebrycian," leaning out of the right line, caught in his left hand the left hand of his adversary, and bringing forth from his side his own huge right one, aimed a blow, which, had it struck where it intended, would have done mischief; but the son of Jove stooped from

---

* 'Αδηφάγον—*Literally*, insatiably eating, voracious; one who has never *had enough*. Observe how the same instinctive phraseology is used by strong sensations all over the world. The " Fancy " pugilistic, and fancy poetical, like differently bred relations, thus find themselves, to their astonishment, of the same family; so the like metaphors of " flashing one's ivories " (for suddenly showing the teeth), " tapping the claret," and other jovial escapes from vulgarity into elegance.

under it, and emerging, gave his enemy such a blow on the left temple as made it spout with blood. He assisted the blow, directly, with another on the mouth, given by the hand which the giant had let drop; and crashing his teeth with the weight of it, followed it with a general clatter on the face, which mashed it a second time, and rendered resistance hopeless. Heavily fell Amycus to the ground, having no more heart, and raising his hands as he fell, in sign of throwing up the contest.

But nothing unbefitting thy worthiness, didst thou inflict, O *pugilist* Polydeuctes, on the conquered. Only he made him take a great oath—calling on his father Neptune out of the sea to witness it—that never more would he do anything grievous to those who sought his hospitality.

It appears to us, reader, and we think it will appear to thee, that even this *prosification* of a fine bit of poetry will afford no disgraceful evidence of the strength and muscle of the gentle shepherd Theocritus. The manner of the concluding passage is quite in the taste of the chivalrous poets of Italy; and forces us to repeat our regret, that the Sicilian left no larger work, to be put at the head of their romances. The *Odyssey*, indeed, is their leader in some respects; but to the grandeur, the wild fictions, and the domestic tenderness of the *Odyssey*, Theocritus would have added the gaiety and good-natured satire of Pulci and Ariosto.

Here follows a specimen (such as it is, and as far as we can pretend to represent the original) of the comic and domestic painting of Theocritus. It is a poem on the *Rites of Adonis* ; or rather, on a couple of gossips, making holiday to enjoy the festival that formed a part of the rites. Adonis, the favourite of Venus, slain by the boar, and permitted by Jupiter to return to life every half-year and enjoy her company, was annually commemorated by the heathen world for the space of two days, the first of which was passed in mourning for his death, and the second, in feasting and merriment for his coming to life. Arsinoe, the consort of the poet's patron, Ptolemy Philadelphus, celebrated these rites in the Egyptian capital, Alexandria ; and Theocritus, in order to praise his royal friends, and at the same time give a picture of his countrywomen, introduces two women who were born in Syracuse and settled in Alexandria, making holiday on the occasion, and going to see the show. The show was that of the second day, and principally consisted of an image of Adonis laid in a bower of leaves and tapestry, and served with all the luxuries of the season, particularly flowers in pots. He was attended by flying Cupids, and eulogized by singers in hymns, much in the manner of saints and angels in a modern Catholic festival; and on the following morning, the image, with its flowers, was taken in procession to the sea-side, and committed to the waters on its way to the other world. The whole proceeding is intimated in the poem, by means of verses put into the mouth of the public singer, the Grisi or Malibran of the day; but the chief portion of it is assigned to the humours of the two gossips, who are precisely such as would be drawn at this moment on a similar occasion in any crowded city. This truth to nature, which is the constant charm of Theocritus (making it, as he does, artistical also with wit and poetry), the reader will recognise at once in the talk about the husband, the endeavours to mystify the little boy, the chatter and bustle in the crowd, and the gaping expressions of delight and amazement at the spectacle. The opening of the poem lets us into a household scene, described with all the nicety and archness of Chaucer.

THE SYRACUSAN GOSSIPS;

OR, THE FEAST OF ADONIS.

GORGO,
PRAXINOE, } *The Gossips.*
EUNOE, *servant of Praxinoe.*
PHRYGIA, *her housemaid.*
Little Boy, her Son.   *Old Woman.*   *Two Men.*

SCENE --*Alexandria in Egypt.*

GORGO. (*at her friend's door.*) Praxinoe within ?
EUNOE.   Why, Gorgo, dear,
How late you are ! Yes, she's within.
PRAX. (*appearing.*)   What, no !
And so you're come at last ! A seat here, Eunoe ;
And set a cushion.
EUNOE.   There is one.
PRAX.   Sit down.
GORGO. Oh, what a thing's a spirit ! Do you know,
I've scarcely got alive to you, Praxinoe ?
There's such a crowd—such heaps of carriages,
And horses, and fine soldiers, all full dress'd ;
And then you live such an immense way off !
PRAX. Why, 'twas *his* shabby doing. He would take
This hole that he calls house, at the world's end.
'Twas all to spite me, and to part us two.
GORGO. (*speaking lower.*) Don't talk so of your husband,
     there's a dear,
Before the little one. See how he looks at you.
PRAX. (*to the little boy.*) There, don't look grave, child :
    cheer up, Zopy, sweet ;

6

It isn't your papa we're talking of.

GORGO. (*aside.*) He thinks it is, though.

PRAX.   Oh no—nice papa!
(*To* GORGO.) Well, this strange body once (let us say *once*,
And then he won't know who we're telling of),
Going to buy some washes and saltpetre,
Comes bringing salt! the great big simpleton!

GORGO. And there's my precious ninny, Dioclede:
He gave for five old ragged fleeces, yesterday,
Ten drachmas!—for mere dirt! trash upon trash!
But come; put on your things; button away,
Or we shall miss the show. It's the king's own;
And I am told the queen has made of it
A wonderful fine thing.

PRAX.   Ay, luck has luck.
Well, tell us all about it; for we hear
Nothing in this vile place.

GORGO.   We haven't time.
Workers can't throw away their holidays.

PRAX. Some water, Eunoe; and then, my fine one,
To take your rest again. Puss loves good lying.
Come; move, girl, move; some water—water first.
Look how she brings it! Now, then;—hold, hold, careless;
Not quite so fast; you're wetting all my gown.
There; that'll do. Now, please the gods, I'm washed.
The key of the great chest—where's that? Go fetch it.

                              [*Exit* EUNOE.

GORGO. Praxinoe, that gown with the full skirts
Becomes you mightily. What did it cost you?

PRAX. Oh, don't remind me of it. More than one
Or two good minas, besides time and trouble.

GORGO. All which you had forgotten.

PRAX.   Ah, ha! True;
That's good. You're quite right.

Re-enter EUNOE.

Come ; my cloak, my cloak ;
And parasol.   There—help it on now, properly.
(*To the little boy.*) Child, child, you cannot go.   The horse
   will bite it ;
The Horrid Woman's coming.   Well, well, simpleton,
Cry, if you will ; but you must not get lamed.
Come, Gorgo.—Phrygia, take the child, and play with him ;
And call the dog indoors, and lock the gate.   [*They go out.*
Powers, what a crowd ! how shall we get along ?
Why, they're like ants ! countless ! innumerable !
Well, Ptolemy, you've done fine things, that's certain,
Since the gods took your father.   No one now-a-days
Does harm to trav'llers as they used to do,
After the Egyptian fashion, lying in wait,—
Masters of nothing but detestable tricks ;
And all alike,—a set of cheats and brawlers.
Gorgo, sweet friend, what will become of us ?
Here are the king's horse-guards !   Pray, my good man,
Don't tread upon us so.   See the bay horse !
Look how it rears !   It's like a great mad dog.
How you stand, Eunoe !   It will throw him certainly !
How lucky that I left the child at home !

   GORGO. Courage, Praxinoe ; they have pass'd us now ;
They've gone into the court-yard.

   PRAX.   Good ! I breathe again.
I never could abide in all my life
A horse and a cold snake.

   GORGO (*addressing an old woman*). From court, mother ?
   OLD WOMAN. Yes, child.
   GORGO.   Pray, is it easy to get in ?
   OLD WOMAN. The Greeks got into Troy.   Everything's
                  done
By trying.   [*Exit* OLD WOMAN.
   GORGO. Bless us !   How she bustles off !

Why, the old woman's quite oracular.
But women must know everything ; ev'n what Juno
Wore on her wedding-day.   See now, Praxinoe,
How the gate's crowded.

PRAX.   Frightfully indeed.
Give me your hand, dear Gorgo ; and do you
Hold fast of Eutychis's, Eunoe.
Don't let her go ; don't stir an inch ; and so
We'll all squeeze in together.   Stick close now.
Oh me! oh me! my veil's torn right in two!
Do take care, my good man, and mind my cloak.

MAN. 'Twas not my fault ; but I'll take care.
PRAX.   What heaps!
They drive like pigs!

MAN.   Courage, old girl! all's safe.
PRAX. Blessings upon you, sir, now and for ever,
For taking care of us—A good, kind soul.
How Eunoe squeezes us!   Do, child, make way
For your own self.   There ; now, we've all got in,
As the man said, when he was put in prison.

GORGO. Praxinoe, do look there!   What lovely tapestry!
How fine and showy!   One would think the gods did it.

PRAX. Holy Minerva! how those artists work!
How they do paint their pictures to the life!
The figures stand so like, and move so like!
They're quite alive, not work'd.   Well, certainly,
Man's a wise creature.   See now—only look—
See—lying on the silver couch, all budding,
With the young down about his face! Adonis!
Charming Adonis—charming ev'n in Acheron!

SECOND MAN. Do hold your tongues there ; chatter,
           chatter, chatter.
The turtles stun one with their yawning gabble.

GORGO. Hey-day!   Whence comes the man ?   What is't
           to you,

If we do chatter ?   Speak where you've a right.
You're not the master here.   And as for that,
Our people are from Corinth, like Bellerophon.
Our tongue's Peloponnesiac ; and we hope
It's lawful for the Dorians to speak Doric !
    PRAX. We've but one master, by the Honey-sweet ! *
And don't fear you, nor all your empty blows.
    GORGO. Hush, hush, Praxinoe !—there's the Grecian
A most amazing creature, going to sing   [girl,
About Adonis ; she that sings so well
The song of Sperchis : she'll sing something fine,
I warrant.—See how sweetly she prepares !

THE SONG.

O Lady, who dost take delight
In Golgos and the Erycian height,
And in the Idalian dell,
Venus, ever amiable ;
Lo, the long-expected Hours,
Slowest of the blessed powers,
Yet who bring us something ever,
Ceasing their soft dancing never,
Bring thee back thy beauteous one
From perennial Acheron.
Thou, they say, from earth hast given
Berenice place in heaven,
Dropping to her woman's heart
Ambrosia ; and for this kind part,
Berenice's daughter —she
That's Helen-like—Arsinoe,
O thou many-named and shrin'd,
Is to thy Adonis kind.
He has all the fruits that now
Hang upon the timely bough :

* An epithet applied by the Sicilians to Proserpine.

He has green young garden-plots,
Basketed in silver pots ;
Syrian scents in alabaster,
And whate'er a curious taster
Could desire, that women make
With oil or honey, of meal cake ;
And all shapes of beast or bird,
In the woods by huntsman stirr'd ;
And a bower to shade his state
Heap'd with dill, an amber weight ;
And about him Cupids flying,
Like young nightingales, that—trying
Their new wings—go half afraid,
Here and there, within the shade.
See the gold !　The ebony see !
And the eagles in ivory,
Bearing the young Trojan up
To be filler of Jove's cup ;
And the tapestry's purple heap,
Softer than the feel of sleep ;
Artists, contradict who can,
Samian or Milesian.
But another couch there is
For Adonis, close to his ;
Venus has it, and with joy
Clasps again her blooming boy
With a kiss that feels no fret,
For his lips are downy yet.
Happy with her love be she ;
But to-morrow morn will we,
With our locks and garments flowing
And our bosoms gently showing,
Come and take him, in a throng,
To the sea-shore, with this song :—
Go, belov'd Adonis, go
Year by year thus to and fro ;

Only privileged demigod ;
There was no such open road
For Atrides ; nor the great
Ajax, chief infuriate ;
Nor for Hector, noblest once
Of his mother's twenty sons ;
Nor Patroclus, nor the boy
That returned from taken Troy ;
Nor those older buried bones,
Lapiths and Deucalions ;
Nor Pelopians, and their boldest ;
Nor Pelasgians, Greece's oldest.
Bless us then, Adonis dear,
And bring us joy another year ;
Dearly hast thou come again,
And dearly shalt be welcomed then.

Gorgo. Well ; if that's not a clever creature, trust me !
Lord ! what a quantity of things she knows !
And what a charming voice !—'Tis time to go, though,
For there's my husband hasn't had his dinner,
And you'd best come across him when he wants it !
Good-by, Adonis, darling. Come again.

CHAPTER V.

THEOCRITUS.—Concluded.

SPECIMENS OF THE PATHOS AND PASTORAL OF THEOCRITUS.
—THE CYCLOPS IN LOVE.—POETICAL FEELING AMONG
UNEDUCATED CLASSES IN THE SOUTH.—PASSAGES FROM
THEOCRITUS'S FIRST IDYLL. — HIS VERSIFICATION AND
MUSIC.— PASTORAL OF BION AND MOSCHUS.

HAVING seen the force and comic humour of Theocritus, let us now, if we can, give something of a taste of his pathos, and conclude with him as the Prince of Pastoral. We shall find the one leading to the other, or rather identified with it, for Polyphemus was himself a shepherd, and all his imagery and associations are drawn from pastoral life. Our English, it is to be borne in mind, is not the

Greek. The poet must have all the benefit of that admission. But at any rate we have done our best not to spoil the original with such artificial modes of speech as destroy all pathos; and feeling has a common language everywhere, which he who is thoroughly moved by it, can never wholly misrepresent.

The story is that of Polyphemus under the circumstances alluded to in our second chapter. It is addressed to the poet's friend Nicias, and is the earliest evidence of that particular personal regard for the medical profession, which is so observable in the history of men of letters; for Nicias was a physician.

THE CYCLOPS IN LOVE.

There is no other medicine against love,
My Nicias, (so at least it seems to me,)
Either to cure it or to calm, but song.
That, that indeed is balmy to men's minds,
And sweet; but 'tis a balm rare to be found;
Though not by you, my friend, who are at once
Physician, and belov'd by all the Nine.

It was by this the Cyclops liv'd among us,
I mean that ancient shepherd, Polypheme,
Who lov'd the sea-nymph, when he budded first
About the lips and curling temples;—lov'd,
Not in the little present-making style,
With baskets of new fruit and pots of roses,
But with consuming passion. Many a time
Would his flocks go home by themselves at eve,

Leaving him wasting by the dark sea-shore ;
And sunrise would behold him wasting still.
Yet ev'n a love like his found balm in verse,
For he would sit, and look along the sea,
And from his rock pipe to some strain like this :—

" O my white love, my Galatea, why
Avoid me thus ?   O whiter than the curd,
Gentler than any lamb, fuller of play
Than kids, yet bitterer than the bright young grape,
You come sometimes, when sweet sleep holds me fast ;
You break away, when sweet sleep lets me loose ;
Gone, like a lamb at sight of the grey wolf.

" Sweet, I began to love you, when you first
Came with my mother to the mountain side
To gather hyacinths.   I show'd the way ;
And then, and afterwards, and to this hour,
I could not cease to love you ; you, who care
Nothing about my love—Great Jove ! no, nothing.

" Fair one, I know why you avoid me thus :
It is because one rugged eyebrow spreads
Across my forehead, solitary and huge,
Shading this eye forlorn.   My nose, too, presses
Flat tow'rds my lip.   And yet, such as I am,
I feed a thousand sheep ; and from them drink
Excellent milk ; and never want for cheese
In summer, nor in autumn, nor dead winter,
Dairies I have, so full.   I can play, too,
Upon the pipe, so as no Cyclops can,
Singing, sweet apple mine, of you and me,
Often till midnight.   And I keep for you
Four bears' whelps, and eleven fawns with collars :
Come to me then, for you shall have them all.

Let the sea rake on the dull shore. Your nights
Would be far sweeter here, well hous'd with me.
The place is beautiful with laurel-trees,
With cypresses, with ivy, and the vine,
The dulcet vine : and here, too, is a stream,
Heavenly to drink, the water is so cold.
The woody Ætna sends it down to me
Out of her pure white snows. Who could have this,
And choose to live in the wild salt-sea waves ?
Perhaps, when I am talking of my trees,
You think me ruder than the trunks ? more rough ;
More rugged-bodied ? Ah, they keep me warm ;
They blaze upon my hearth ; yet, I could lose
Warmth, life, and all, and burn in the same fire,
Rather than dwell beside it without you.
Nay, I could burn the eye from out my head,
Though nothing else be dearer.

                       "Oh, poor me !
Alas ! that I was born a finless body,
And cannot dive to you, and kiss your hand ;
Or, if you grudg'd me that, bring you white lilies,
And the fresh poppy with its thin red leaves.
And yet not so ; for poppies grow in summer,
Lilies in spring ; and so I could not, both.
But should some coaster, sweetest, in his ship
Come here to see me, I would learn to swim ;
And then I might find out what joy there is
In living, as you do, in the dark deeps.
  "O Galatea, that you would but come ;
And having come, forget, as I do now,
Here where I sat me, to go home again !
You should keep sheep with me, and milk the dams,
And press the cheese from the sharp-tasted curd.
  is my mother that's to blame. She never
Told you one kind, endearing thing of me,

Though she has seen me wasting day by day.
My very head and feet, for wretchedness,
Throb—and so let 'em ; for I too am wretched.
O Cyclops, Cyclops, where are thy poor senses ?
Go to thy basket-making ; get their supper
For the young lambs. 'Twere wiser in thee, far.
Prize what thou hast, and let the lost sheep go.
Perhaps thou'lt find another Galatea,
Another, and a lovelier ; for at night
Many girls call to me to come and play,
And when they find me list'ning, they all giggle
So that e'en I seem counted somebody."

    Thus Polyphemus medicined his love
With pipe and song ; and found it ease him more
Than all the balms he might have bought with gold.

What say you, reader ? Is not the monster touching ? Do we not accord with his self-pity ? feel for his throbbing pulse and his hopeless humility, and wish it were possible for a beauty to love a shepherd with one eye ?—For the poet, observe, with great address, has said nothing about the giant. He has sunk the man-mountain. We may rate him at what equivocal measure we please, and consider him a respectable primæval sort of pastoral Orson. It appears to us, that there is no truer pathos of its kind in the whole circle of poetry than the passages about the sheep and wolf, the throbbing pulses just mentioned, and the lover's humble attempt to get a little consolation of vanity out of the equivocal interest taken in him by the "giggling" damsels at the foot of his hill. The word "giggle," which is the literal translation of the Greek word, and singularly like it in the main sound, would have been thought very bold by a conventional poet. Not so thought the poet whose truth to nature has made him immortal.

We are to fancy the Sicilian girls on a summer night (all the world is out of door there on summer nights) calling to Polyphemus up the mountain. They live at the foot of it—of Ætna. They have heard him stirring in the trees. The stir ceases. They know he is listening; and in the silence of the glen below, he hears them laughing at his attention. Such scenes take place all over the world, where there is any summer, Britain included. We doubt whether Virgil or Tasso would have ventured upon the word. But Ariosto would. Homer and Shakspeare would. So would Dante. So would Catullus, a very Greek man. And it would surely not have been avoided by the author of the *Gentle Shepherd*, whose perception of homely truth puts him on a par in this respect with the greatest truth poetical.

This love-story of Polyphemus is pastoral poetry in its highest passionate condition. Of pastoral, in the sense in which it is generally understood, a briefer or better specimen cannot be given than in the opening passages of our poet's volume. You are in the circle of pastoral at once, and in one of its loveliest spots. You are in the open air under pine-trees by fountain-heads, in company with two born poets, goatherd and shepherd though they be; poets such as Burns and Allan Ramsay might have been, had they been born in Sicily.

A word, before we proceed, in respect to that inter-fusion of eloquent and therefore sometimes elegant expression which has been charged on one of the most natural of poets as an affectation, but which, as *he* treats it, is only in unison with the popular genius of the south. In Virgil it became a rhetorical mistake; an artificial flower stuck in the ground. In Theocritus it was the growth of the soil; myrtle and almond spring-ing by the wayside.

Poetical expression in humble life is to be found all over the south. In the instances of Burns, Ramsay, and others, the north also has seen it. Indeed, it is not a little remarkable, that Scotland, which is more northern than England, and possesses not even a night-ingale, has had more of it than its southern neighbour. What that is owing to, is a question; perhaps to the very restrictions of John Knox and his fellows, and Nature's happy tendency to counteract them. Or it may

have originated in the wild and uncertain habits of
highlanders and borderers. Certainly, the Scotch have
shown a more genial and impulsive spirit in their songs
and dances than the English. We have nothing among
us like the Highland Fling, or the reel of Tulloch-
gorum, or the songs of *Gaberlunzie Men*, *Jolly
Beggars*, and *The gude man he cam' hame at e'en*.
But extremes meet; and the Scotch, in their hardi-
hood, their very poverty, and occasional triumphs over it
in fits of excess, appear to have been driven by a jovial
desperation into the vivacities inspired by the sunshine
of the south. Yet the Irish are a still greater puzzle in
this respect; for they are poorer; their land is in the
English latitude; and nevertheless the poetical feeling
is far more common and more eloquent among them,
than with either of their neighbours. Their fertility of
fancy and readiness of expression render them, in fact,
very like a southern people; and, if a doubt, alas! did
not arise that misfortune itself was their inspirer by
sharpening their sensibility, would give an almost
laughable corroboration to their claims of a Milesian
descent. Now, the Italian peasantry to this day,
particularly the Tuscan, exhibit, as they always did, a
like poetical fancy, but with more elegance; and so, we
doubt not, did those of Greece and Sicily. The latter,
in modern times, have been checked in their faculties by

unfavourable government; but in the time of Theocritus, the subjects of the overflowingly rich cities of Syracuse and Agrigentum must have been as willing and able to pour out all they felt, as so many well-fed thrushes and blackbirds; and anybody at all acquainted with the less rich, but not ill-governed, Tuscan peasantry, knows well with how much eloquence, and even refinement, it is possible for people in humble life to express themselves, when the language is favourable, and circumstances not otherwise. Mr. Stewart Rose has given some amusing instances in his *Letters from the North of Italy.* Asking a Florentine servant if he understood some directions given him, the man said, "Yes, for he always spoke in relief" ("Che parlava sempre scolpito"). Nothing could be better expressed than this. Another time, his good-natured master, inquiring if he was comfortable on the coach-box, the servant answered that he was very well off; for "here," said he, "one springs it" ("che qui si molleggia"). The verb was coined for the occasion from the noun *molla*, a spring. Another man being asked the way to a particular house, told him to go straight forwards to the end of the street, and it would "tumble on his head." This is very Irish. An Italian acquaintance of Mr. Rose was passing through a street in Florence at serenade time, when he beheld a dog looking up at a female of his species in a balcony,

and at the same time scratching his ribs. One of the
Florentine populace, who happened to be passing,
stopped, and cried out, "He is in love, and playing the
guitar, serenading the fair one" ("È innamorato; suona
la chitarra; fà la cucchiata alla bella"). A Roman
laquais de place (but he is a more sophisticate
authority) once asked the same writer, on seeing him
look at a wild-flower in the fields, whether it was the
signor's "pleasure that he should cull it?" ("Commanda
che lo carpa?") For our poetical word "cull," though
its meaning is different, may represent the unvernacular
elegance of *carpa*, pluck. The laquais de place, it
seems, "talked like a cardinal." We have ourselves, however, heard a coachman's wife, who was a Roman, pour
forth a stream of elegant language that astonished us.

A neighbour of ours, near Fiesole, a fine old Tuscan
peasant, who was clipping a hedge, said to us one day,
as we exchanged salutation with him, "I am trimming
the bush's beard" ("Fò la barba al bosco"). But a Florentine female servant, who had the child of an acquaintance
in her arms, and who, like the generality of her countrywomen, was perfectly unaffected, carried the aristocratic
refinement of her style higher, perhaps, than any of the
persons mentioned. Some remarks being made respecting the countenances of her master's children, she asked
us whether the one in her arms did not form an excep-

7

tion; whether, in fact, we did not think that it had "a kind of plebeian look" ("un certo aspetto plebeo").

So much for the ability of the humbler orders to speak with force and delicacy, when sensibility gives them the power of expression, and animal spirits the courage to use it.

PASSAGES FROM THE FIRST IDYLL OF THEOCRITUS.

In Theocritus's opening poem, the time of day is a hot noon, and a shepherd and goatherd appear to have been piping under their respective trees, we suppose at a reasonable distance. The shepherd goes towards the goatherd, who seems to stop playing; and on approaching him commences the dialogue by observing, that there is something extremely pleasant in the whisper of the pine under which he is sitting, but not less so was the something he was playing just now on his pipe. He declares that he is the next best player after Pan himself; and that if Pan were to have a ram for his prize, the ewe would of necessity fall to the goatherd.

> Sweet sings the rustling of your pine to-day
> Over the fountain-heads; and no less sweet
> Upon the pipe play you.

The Greek word for rustling, or rather whispering— *psithurisma*—is much admired. "Whispering" is hardly strong enough, and not so long drawn out. There is the continuous whisper in *psithurisma*. The goatherd returns the compliment by telling the shepherd that his singing during such hot weather (for we must always keep in mind the accessories implied by good poets) is sweeter than the flowing abundance of the waterfall out of the rock. The two verses in which this is expressed are a favourite quotation, on account of the imitative beauty of the second sentence. We know not whether they would equally please every critical ear, for " doctors," even of music, " differ." Much of the divine writing of Beethoven seems to have been as appalling at first to the orchestral world, as olives are to most palates; and there is a passage in Mozart which to this day is a choke-pear to the scientific, albeit they acknowledge that he intended it to be written as it stands. For our parts, we have great faith in the ultra-delights perceptible in the enormities of Beethoven, Mozart, and olives; and suspect there is more music in the very hissing and clatter in the sentence in Theocritus, to say nothing of its obvious rush and leaping, than has been quite perceived by every scholar who has praised it. It is a pity that all musical people do not read Greek; for they deserve to do so ; which is what cannot be said of all scholars. Perhaps some of them would be glad to see the passage, even in English characters.

We remember, before we knew any others, the delight we used to take in the Greek quotations, thus printed in the novels of Smollett and Fielding, and shall make no further apology for a like bit of typography. We shall first give the measure of the original verse in corresponding English hexameters. The English language does not take kindly to the measure. The hexameter is too salient and cantering for it. But once and away the anomaly may be tolerated, especially for illustration's sake. The passage in English words may run thus :—

Sweeter, O shepherd, thy singing is, than the sonorous
Gush from above of the waterfall out of the rock-stone.

There is no imitative attempt of another sort in this version. It is given simply to show a general likeness to the measure. The sound of the original, as everybody will discern, is much more to the purpose, though judges will differ perhaps as to whether it is more effective in softness or in strength, in leap or in volume. We are obliged to adapt the spelling, in one or two instances, to the necessities of the pronunciation. The literal Greek order of the words would, in English, be :—

Sweeter, O shepherd, the thy song, than the sonorous
That (or yonder) from the rock-stone much flows from above water.

Hàdion o poiman to teòn melos è to katàches
Teen appo tas pètras katalèibetai hèupsothen hèudor.

Kataleibetai (much, or strongly, or abundantly, flows), with the accent on the diphthong *ei*, is certainly a fine strenuous word, at once strong and liquid, and appreciable by any ear. And *hèupsothen hèudor* (from above water), with its two successive *u*'s, will be equally admitted, we think, to express the constant *yearning* rush of the water from inside the well.

The goatherd promises the shepherd, if he will sing to him, the gift of a huge wine-cup, adorned with figures. The following exquisite picture is among them. We give it in the version of Mr. M. J. Chapman, a living writer, not unworthy his venerable namesake, and by far the best translator of Theocritus that has appeared :—

Ἔντοσθεν δὲ γυνὰ, &c.

With flowing robe, and Lydian head-dress on,
Within, a woman to the life is done—
An exquisite design ! On either side
Two men with flowing locks each other chide,
By turns contending for the woman's love ;
But not a whit her mind their pleadings move :
One while she gives to this a glance and smile,
And turns and smiles on that another while.

To the apparently formidable objection made by some critics, that no artist could make a woman look on two people one after the other, Mr. Chapman happily answers :—" Theocritus described an image that was before his mind's eye, and for so doing he needs no

defence; but the matter-of-fact critic may be able,
perhaps, to obtain an approximation to the idea, by
considering attentively the print of 'Garrick divided
between Tragedy and Comedy.'" *

This picture is followed by one of an old able-bodied
fisherman at his labours, with the muscles of his neck
swelling like those of a strong young man; and to this
succeeds a third, as good as that of the Coquette—some
will think better. It is a boy so intent upon making a
trap, that he is not aware of the presence of two foxes,
one of whom is meditating to abduct his breakfast.

> A little boy sits by the thorn-edge trim,
> To watch the grapes—two foxes watching *him*;

(The version of this line is original in the turn of it,
and very happy.)

> One through the ranges of the vine proceeds,
> And on the hanging vintage slily feeds;
> The other plots and vows his scrip to search,
> And for his breakfast leave him in the lurch.

> Meanwhile he twines, and to a rush fits well
> A locust-trap, with stalks of asphodel;
> And twines away with such absorbing glee,
> Of scrip or vines he never thinks, not he!
> CHAPMAN, p. 8.

* *The Greek Pastoral Poets, Theocritus, Bion, and Moschus, done
into English by M. J. Chapman, M.A., of Trinity College, Cambridge,*
pp. 7, 331.--We like the good faith of Mr. Chapman's "done into
English."

In the pastorals of Bion we know nothing of prominent interest, though he is eloquent and worth reading. But in those of Moschus there is a passage which has found an echo in all bosoms, like the sigh that answers a wind over a churchyard. It is in the Elegy on Bion's death :—

Αἴ, αἴ, ταὶ μαλάχαι μέν ἐπὰν κατὰ κᾶπον ὀλώνται,
Ἢ τὰ χλωρὰ σέλινα, τὸ τ' εὐθαλες οὖλον ἄνηθον,
Ὕστερον αὖ ζώοντι, καὶ εἰσ ἔτος ἄλλο φύοντι·
Ἄμμες δ' οἱ μεγάλοι, καὶ καρτέροι, ἢ σόφοι ἄνδρες,
Ὁππότε πρᾶτα θάνωμες, ἀνακύοι ἕν χθονὶ κοῖλα,
Εὕδομες εὖ μάλα μακρὸν, ἀτέρμονα, νήγρετον ὕπνον.

Idyll iii. v. 104.

Alas! when mallows in the garden die,
Green parsley, or the crisp luxuriant dill,
They live again, and flower another year ;
But we, how great soe'er, or strong, or wise,
When once *we* die, sleep, in the senseless earth,
A long, an endless, unawakeable sleep.

The beautiful original of these verses, every word so natural and sincere, so well placed, and the whole so affecting, may stand by the side of any poetry, even that of the passage in the Book of Job too well known to most of us. But we confess that after such Greek verses as these, and the fresh flowers of Theocritus, we never have the heart to quote the artificial ones of Virgil, critically accomplished as they are. They are the pattern of too many others which brought the word

Pastoral into disrepute; and it is not pleasant to be forced to object to a great name.

Virgil, however, appears to have been very fond of the country; and after he was settled in Rome, longed for it, like Horace, with a feeling which produced some of his most admired passages; things which other metropolitan poets and tired court gentlemen have delighted to translate.   Such are the *Delights of a Country Life*, versified out of the *Georgics* by Cowley, Sir William Temple, Dryden, and others, lines of which remain for ever in the memory.

> Oh happy (*if his happiness he knows*)
> The country swain, &c.

He has no great riches, or visitors, or cares, &c., but his life

> Does with substantial blessedness abound,
> *And the soft wings of peace cover him round.*

That is Cowley, who betters his original.

> In life's cool vale let my low scene be laid;
> *Cover me, gods! with Tempe's thickest shade.*

So again of the shepherd :—

> —In th' evening of a fair sunny day,
> With joy he sees his flocks and kids to play,
> And loaded kine about his cottage stand,
> Inviting with known sound the milker's hand;
> And when from wholesome labour he doth come,
> With wishes to be there, and wish'd for home,

He meets at door the softest human blisses,
His chaste wife's welcome, and dear children's kisses.

Of a similar kind is Cowley's translation of Claudian's *Old Man of Verona* :—

Happy the man who his whole time doth bound
Within th' enclosure of his little ground.—
Him no false distant lights, by fortune set,
Could ever into foolish wanderings get ;—
No change of consuls marks to him the year :
The change of seasons is his calendar :
The cold and heat winter and summer shows ;
Autumn by fruits, and spring by flow'rs, he knows :—
A neighb'ring wood born with himself he sees,
And loves his old contemporary trees.

The most original bit of Pastoral in Virgil (if it be his) is to be found in a poem of doubtful authority called the *Gnat* (Culex), which has been beautifully translated by Spenser. It is a true picture, combining the elegance of Claude with the minuteness of the Flemish painters :—

The fiery sun was mounted now on height
    Up to the heavenly towers, and shot each where
Out of his golden charet glistering light ;
    And fayre Aurora, with her rosie haire,
The hatefull darkness now had put to flight ;
    When as the shepherd, seeing day appeare,
His little goats gan drive out of their stalls,
To feede abroad, where pasture best befalls.

To an high mountain's top he with them went,
    Where thickest grasse did cloath the open hills :

They, now amongst the woods and thicketts ment,
  Now in the vallies wandring at their wills,
Spread themselves farre abroad through each descent;
  Some on the soft green grasse feeding their fills;
Some, clambering through the hollow cliffes on hy,
Nibble the bushie shrubs which growe thereby.

Others the utmost boughs of trees doe crop,
  And brouze the woodbine twigges that freshly bud;
This with full bit doth catch the utmost top
  Of some soft willow or new-growen stud;
That with sharpe teeth the bramble leaves doth lop,
  And chaw the tender prickles in her cud;
The whiles another high doth overlooke
Her own like image in a cristall brook.

This is picturesque and charming. Yet Virgil,
though a country-loving, and also an agricultural poet,
would have been nothing as a pastoral poet without
Theocritus, and, as it was, he spoiled him. We shall
see in what manner, when we come to speak of Pope.

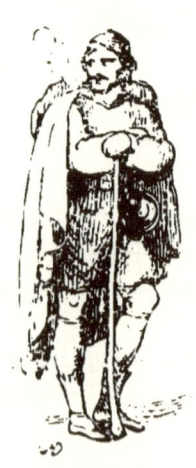

CHAPTER VI.

NORMAN TIMES—LEGEND OF KING ROBERT.

HOW KING ROBERT OF SICILY WAS DISPOSSESSED OF HIS
THRONE ; AND WHO SAT UPON IT.—HIS WRATH, SUFFER-
INGS, AND REPENTANCE.

IN the glance at the anci- ent history of Sicily in our third chapter, we have seen that the Greek and Roman sway was succeeded by that of the Sara- cens. They were masters of the island for the space of two hundred years, but have left no memorials, with the exception of a building or two, and traces of Arabic in the Sicilian tongue. The island was then conquered by a handful of Norman gentlemen, who had obtained possession of Naples, and whose history would be romantic enough to be worth repeating, if it were anything but a succession of wars. Their wonderful ascendency, and no less extraordinary personal prowess, are supposed by some, not without reason, to have given rise to much of the gigantic fable of the Orlandos and other peers of Charlemagne, who were all Frenchmen.

As an old ruin, therefore, standing in some spot surrounded by architecture of different orders, will sometimes be found to be the sole representative of a former age, we shall make the good old legend of King Robert, in this our Sicilian and Pastoral Sketch-book, stand for the whole Norman portion of its chronology. It is not military, except in the *brusque* self-sufficiency with which the character of King Robert sets out; but it is emphatically what we understand by Gothic; which, in modern parlance, implies the character of the interval between ancient and modern times. The Greek Sicilian poets, could they have foreseen it, would have loved it; and their successors, the pastoral writers of modern times, of whom we have afterwards to speak, unquestionably did so, whenever they met with it among their old reading. Shakspeare would have made a divine play of it, for it is very dramatic. Fancy what he would have done with the angel, and the court fool, and the pathos! Oh, that we had had but time to try even to dramatize it ourselves.

Who King Robert of Sicily may have been, in common earthly history—whether intended to shadow forth one of the aforesaid Norman chieftains who obtained possession of that island, or one of the various dukes who contend for the honour of being called Robert the Devil, or whether he was Robert of Anjou, hight Robert the Wise, the friend of Petrarch and Boccaccio, and father of the calumniated Joanna—we must leave to antiquaries to determine. Suffice to say, that in history angelical, and in the depths of one of the very finest kinds of truth, he was King Robert of Sicily, brother of Pope Urban, and of the Emperor *Valemond*. A like story has been told of the Emperor *Jovinian* (whoever that prince may have been); and we shall not dispute that something of the kind may have occurred to him also; since very strange things happen to the most haughty of princes, if we did but know their whole lives; not excepting their being taken for fools by their people. We shall avail ourselves of any light which the histories of the king and the emperor may serve to throw on each other.

Writers, then, inform us, that King Robert of Sicily, brother of Pope Urban and of the Emperor

Valemond, was a prince of great courage and renown, but of a temper so proud and impatient, that he did not choose to bend his knee to Heaven itself, but would sit twirling his beard, and looking with something worse than indifference round about him, during the gravest services of the church.

One day, while he was present at vespers on the eve of St. John, his attention was excited to some words in the Magnificat, in consequence of a sudden dropping of the choristers' voices. The words were these. " *Deposuit potentes de sede, et exaltavit humiles.*" ("He hath put down the mighty from their seat, and hath exalted the humble." Being far too great and warlike a prince to know anything about Latin, he asked a chaplain near him the meaning of these words; and being told what it was, observed, that such expressions were no better than an old song, since men like himself were not so easily put down, much less supplanted by poor creatures whom people call " humble."

The chaplain, doubtless out of pure astonishment and horror, made no reply; and his majesty, partly from the heat of the weather, and partly to relieve himself from the rest of the service, fell asleep.

After some lapse of time, the royal " sitter in the seat of the scornful," owing, as he thought, to the sound of the organ, but in reality to a great droning fly in his ear, woke up in more than his usual state of impatience; and he was preparing to vent it, when, to his astonishment, he perceived the church empty. Every soul was gone, excepting a deaf old woman who was turning up the cushions. He addressed her to no purpose; he spoke louder and louder, and was proceeding, as well as rage and amaze would let him, to try if he could walk out of the church without a dozen lords before him, when, suddenly catching a sight of his face, the old woman uttered a cry of "Thieves!" and shuffling away, closed the door behind her.

King Robert looked at the door in silence, then round about him at the empty church, then at himself. His cloak of ermine was gone. The coronet was taken from his cap. The very jewels from his fingers. "Thieves, verily!" thought the king, turning white from shame and rage. "Here is conspiracy—rebellion! This is that sanctified traitor, the duke. Horses shall tear them all to pieces. What, ho, there! Open the door for the king!"

"For the constable, you mean," said a voice through the key-hole. "You're a pretty fellow!"

The king said nothing.

"Thinking to escape, in the king's name," said the voice, "after hiding to plunder his closet. We've got you."

Still the king said nothing.

The sexton could not refrain from another jibe at his prisoner :

"*I* see you there," said he, " by the big lamp, grinning like a rat in a trap. How do you like your bacon ? "

Now, whether King Robert was of the blood of that Norman chief who felled his enemy's horse with a blow of his fist, we know not ; but certain it is, that the only answer he made the sexton was by dashing his enormous foot against the door, and bursting it open in his teeth. The sexton, who felt as if a house had given him a blow in the face, fainted away ; and the king, as far as his sense of dignity allowed him, hurried to his palace, which was close by.

" Well," said the porter, " what do *you* want ? "

" Stand aside, fellow ! " roared the king, pushing back the door with the same gigantic foot.

" Go to the devil ! " said the porter, who was a stout fellow too, and pushed the king back before he expected resistance. The king, however, was too much for him. He felled him to the ground; and half strode, half rushed into the palace, followed by the exasperated janitor.

" Seize him ! " cried the porter.

" On your lives ! " cried the king. " Look at me, fellow :—who am I ? "

"A mad beast and fool; that's what you are," cried the porter; "and you're a dead man for coming drunk into the palace, and hitting the king's servants. Hold him fast."

In came the guards, with an officer at their head, who was going to visit his mistress, and had been dressing his curls at a looking-glass. He had the looking-glass in his hand.

"Captain Francavilla," said the king, "is the world run mad? or what is it? Do your rebels pretend not even to know me? Go before me, sir, to my rooms." And as he spoke, the king shook off his assailants, as a lion does curs, and moved onwards.

Captain Francavilla put his finger gently before the king to stop him; and then looking with a sort of staring indifference in his face, said in a very mincing tone, "Some madman."

King Robert tore the looking-glass from the captain's hand, and looked himself in the face. *It was not his own face.* It was another man's face, very hot and vulgar; and had something in it at once melancholy and ridiculous.

"By the living God!" exclaimed Robert, "here is witchcraft! I am changed." And, for the first time in his life, a sensation of fear came upon him, but nothing so great as the rage and fury that remained.

All the world believed in witchcraft, as well as King Robert; but they had still more certain proofs of the existence of drunkenness and madness. The royal household had seen the king come forth from church as usual; and they were ready to split their sides for laughter at the figment of this raving impostor, pretending to be his majesty *changed* !

" Bring him in—bring him in ! " now exclaimed other voices, the news having got to the royal apartments; " the king wants to see him."

King Robert was brought in ; and there, amidst roars of laughter (for courts were not quite such well-bred places then as they are now), he found himself face to face with *another King Robert*, seated on his throne, and as like his former self as he himself was unlike, but with more dignity.

" Hideous impostor ! " exclaimed Robert, rushing forward to tear him down.

The court, at the word " hideous," roared with greater laughter than before ; for the king, in spite of his pride, was at all times a handsome man ; and there was a strong feeling at present, that he had never in his life looked so well.

Robert, when half way to the throne, felt as if a palsy had smitten him. He stopped, and essayed to vent his rage, but could not speak.

The figure on the throne looked him steadily in the face. Robert thought it was a wizard, but hated far more than he feared it; for he was of great courage.

It was an Angel.

But the Angel was not going to disclose himself yet, nor for a long time. Meanwhile, he behaved, on the occasion, very much like a man; we mean, like a man of ordinary feelings and resentments, though still mixed with a dignity beyond what had been before observed in the Sicilian monarch. Some of the courtiers attributed it to a sort of royal instinct of contrast, excited by the claims of the impostor; but others (by the Angel's contrivance) had seen him, as he came out of the church, halt suddenly, with an abashed and altered visage, before the shrine of St. Thomas, as if supernaturally struck with some visitation from Heaven for his pride and unbelief. The rumour flew about on the instant, and was confirmed by an order given from the throne, the moment the Angel seated himself upon it, for a gift of hitherto unheard-of amount to the shrine itself.

" Since thou art royal-mad," said the new sovereign, "and in truth a very king of idiots, thou shalt be crowned and sceptred with a cap and bauble, and be my fool."

Robert was still tongue-tied. He tried in vain to

speak—to roar out his disgust and defiance ; and half
mad, indeed, with the inability, pointed with his
quivering finger to the inside of his mouth, as if in
apology to the beholders for not doing it. Fresh shouts
of laughter made his brain seem to reel within him.

"Fetch the cap and bauble," said the sovereign,
"and let the King of Fools have his coronation."

Robert felt that he must submit to what he thought
the power of the devil. He began even to have glimpses
of a real though hesitating sense of the advantage of
securing friendship on the side of Heaven. But rage
and indignation were uppermost ; and while the attendants were shaving his head, fixing the cap, and jeeringly
dignifying him with the bauble-sceptre, he was racking
his brain for schemes of vengeance. What exasperated
him most of all, next to the shaving, was to observe,
that those who had flattered him most when a king,
were the loudest in their contempt, now that he was the
court-zany. One pompous lord in particular, with a high
and ridiculous voice, which continued to laugh when
all the rest had done, and produced fresh peals by the
continuance, was so excessively provoking, that Robert,
who felt his vocal and muscular powers restored to him
as if for the occasion, could not help shaking his fist at
the grinning slave, and crying out, " Thou beast, Terranova ! " which, in all but the person so addressed, only

produced additional merriment. At length, the king ordered the fool to be taken away, in order to sup with the dogs. Robert was stupefied ; but he found himself hungry against his will, and gnawed the bones which had been chucked away by his nobles.

The proud King Robert of Sicily lived in this way for two years, always raging in his mind, always sullen in his manners, and subjected to every indignity which his quondam favourites could heap on him, without the power to resent it. For the new monarch seemed unjust to him only. He had all the humiliations, without any of the privileges, of the cap and bells, and was the dullest fool ever heard of. All the notice the king took of him consisted in his asking, now and then, in full court, when everything was silent, " Well, fool, art thou still a king ? " Robert, for some weeks, loudly answered that he was ; but, finding that the answer was but a signal for a roar of laughter, he converted his speech into the silent dignity of a haughty and royal attitude ; till, observing that the laughter was greater at this dumb show, he ingeniously adopted a manner which expressed neither defiance nor acquiescence, and the Angel for some time let him alone.

Meantime, everybody but the unhappy Robert blessed the new, or, as they supposed him, the altered king : for everything in the mode of government was changed.

Taxes were light; the poor had plenty; work was reasonable; the nobles themselves were expected to work
after their fashion—to study, to watch zealously over the
interests of their tenants, to travel, to bring home new
books and innocent luxuries. Half the day throughout
Sicily was given to industry, and half to healthy and
intellectual enjoyment; and the inhabitants became
at once the manliest and tenderest, the gayest and most
studious people in the world. Wherever the king went,
he was loaded with benedictions; and the fool heard
them, and began to wonder *what the devil* the devil had
to do with appearances so extraordinary. And thus, for
the space of time we have mentioned, he lived wondering, and sullen, and hating, and hated, and despised.

At the expiration of these two years, or nearly so,
the king announced his intention of paying a visit to his
brother the Pope and his brother the Emperor, the
latter agreeing to come to Rome for the purpose. He
went accordingly with a great train, clad in the most
magnificent garments, all but the fool, who was arrayed
in fox-tails, and put side by side with an ape, dressed
like himself. The people poured out of their houses,
and fields, and vineyards, all struggling to get a sight
of the king's face, and to bless it; the ladies strewing
flowers, and the peasants' wives holding up their rosy
children, which last sight seemed particularly to delight

the sovereign. The fool, bewildered, came after the court pages, by the side of his ape, exciting shouts of laughter; though some persons were a little astonished to think how a monarch so kind and considerate to all the rest of the world, should be so hard upon a sorry fool. But it was told them, that this fool was the most perverse and insolent of men towards the prince himself; and then, although their wonder hardly ceased, it was full of indignation against the unhappy wretch, and he was loaded with every kind of scorn and abuse. The proud King Robert seemed the only blot and disgrace upon the island.

The fool had still a hope, that when his Holiness the Pope saw him, the magician's arts would be at an end; for though he had had no religion at all, properly speaking, he had retained something even of a superstitious faith in the highest worldly form of it. The good Pope, however, beheld him without the least recognition; so did the Emperor; and when he saw them both gazing with unfeigned admiration at the exalted beauty of his former altered self, and not with the old faces of pretended good-will and secret dislike, a sense of awe and humility, for the first time, fell gently upon him. Instead of getting as far as possible from his companion the ape, he approached him closer and closer, partly that he might shroud himself under the very

shadow of his insignificance, partly from a feeling of
absolute sympathy, and a desire to possess, if not one
friend in the world, at least one associate who was not
an enemy.

It happened that day, that it was the same day on
which, two years ago, Robert had scorned the words in
the Magnificat. Vespers were performed before the
sovereigns : the music and the soft voices fell softer as
they came to the words ; and Robert again heard, with
far different feelings, " He hath put down the mighty
from their seat, and exalted the humble." Tears gushed
into his eyes, and, to the astonishment of the court, the
late brutal fool was seen with his hands clasped upon
his bosom in prayer, and the water pouring down his
face in floods of penitence. Holier feelings than usual
had pervaded all hearts that day. The king's favourite
chaplain had preached from the text which declares
charity to be greater than faith or hope. The Emperor
began to think mankind really his brothers. The Pope
wished that some new council of the church would
authorise him to set up, instead of the Jewish Ten
Commandments, and in more glorious letters, the new,
eleventh, or great Christian commandment,—" Behold
I give unto you a *new* commandment, LOVE ONE
ANOTHER." In short, Rome felt that day like angel-
governed Sicily.

When the service was over, the unknown King Robert's behaviour was reported to the unsuspected King-Angel, who had seen it but said nothing. The sacred interloper announced his intention of giving the fool his discharge; and he sent for him accordingly, having first dismissed every other person. King Robert came in his fool's cap and bells, and stood humbly at a distance before the strange great charitable unknown, looking on the floor and blushing. He had the ape by the hand, who had long courted his good-will, and who, having now obtained it, clung to his human friend in a way that, to a Roman, might have seemed ridiculous, but to the Angel, was affecting.

"Art thou still a king?" said the Angel, putting the old question, but without the word "fool."

"I am a fool," said King Robert, "and no king."

"What wouldst thou, Robert?" returned the Angel, in a mild voice.

King Robert trembled from head to foot, and said, "Even what thou wouldst, O mighty and good stranger, whom I know not how to name,—hardly to look at!"

The stranger laid his hand on the shoulder of King Robert, who felt an inexpressible calm suddenly diffuse itself over his being. He knelt down, and clasped his hands to thank him.

"Not to me," interrupted the Angel, in a grave, but

sweet voice; and kneeling down by the side of Robert, he said, as if in church, " Let us pray."

King Robert prayed, and the Angel prayed, and after a few moments, the king looked up, and the Angel was gone; and then the king knew that it was an Angel indeed.

And his own likeness returned to King Robert, but never an atom of his pride; and after a blessed reign, he died, disclosing this history to his weeping nobles, and requesting that it might be recorded in the Sicilian Annals.

CHAPTER VII.

ITALIAN AND ENGLISH PASTORAL.

HE best pastoral is often written when the author least intends it. A completer feeling of the country and of a shepherd's life is given us in a single passage of the *Jerusalem Delivered,*

where Erminia finds herself among a set of peaceful villagers, than in the whole *Aminta*—beautiful, too, as the latter is in many respects, and containing the divine ode on the Golden Age, the crown of all pastoral aspiration. That, indeed, carries everything, even truth itself, before it; saving the truth of man's longing after a state of happiness compatible with his desires. The first line of it, the most beautiful of sighs, is familiar as a proverb in the lips of Italy, and of the lovers of Italy :—

O bella età de l'oro !
Non già perchè di latte
Sen corse il fiume, e stillò mele il bosco ;
Non perchè i frutti loro
Dier da l' aratro intatte
Le terre, e i serpi errar senz' ira o tosco ;
Non perchè nuvol fosco
Non spiegò allor suo velo,
Ma in primavera eterna
Ch' ora s' accende, e verna,
Rise di luce e di sereno il cielo,
Nè portò peregrino
O guerra o merce a gli altrui lidi il pino.

Ma sol perchè quel vano
Nome senza soggetto,
Quell' idolo d' errori, idol d' inganno,
Quel che dal volgo insano
Onor poscia fù detto,
Che di nostra natura il feo tiranno,
Non mischiava il suo affanno
Fra le liete dolcezze

De l' amoroso gregge ;
Nè fu sua dura legge
Nota a quell' alme in libertate avvezze :
Ma legge aurea e felice,
Che natura scolpì,—s' ei piace, ei lice.

O lovely age of gold !
Not that the rivers roll'd
With milk, or that the woods wept honey-dew ;
Not that the ready ground
Produced without a wound,
Or the mild serpent had no tooth that slew ;
Not that a cloudless blue
For ever was in sight,
Or that the heaven, which burns
And now is cold by turns,
Look'd out in glad and everlasting light ;
No, nor that even the insolent ships from far
Brought war to no new lands, nor riches worse than
    war.

But solely that that vain
And breath-invented pain,
That idol of mistake, that worshipp'd cheat,
That Honour—since so call'd
By vulgar minds appall'd,
Play'd not the tyrant with our nature yet.
It had not come to fret
The sweet and happy fold
Of gentle human-kind ;
Nor did its hard law bind
Souls nursed in freedom ; but that law of gold,
That glad and golden law, all free, all fitted,
Which nature's own hand wrote—What pleases, is
    permitted.

Guarini, who wrote his *Pastor Fido* in emulation of
the *Aminta*, undertook to show that these regrets were
immoral, and agreeably to an Italian fashion, made at
once a grave rebuke and a literal rhyming parody of the
original, in an ode beginning with the same words, and
repeating most of them ! His version of "What pleases,
is permitted," is " Take pleasure, if permitted ! " as if
Tasso did not know all about that side of the question,
and was not prepared to be quite as considerate in his
moral conduct and his discountenance of rakes and
seducers as Guarini : whose poem, after all, incurred
charges of licence and temptation, from which that of
his prototype was free ;—an old conventional story !
All which Tasso did, was to put into the mouths of his
shepherds, themselves an ideal people, a wish which is
felt by the whole world—namely, that duty and incli-
nation could be more reconciled to innocence than they
are ; and the world has shown that it agreed with his
honest sighs, and not with the pick-thank commonplaces of his reprover ; for it has treasured his beautiful ode in its memory, and forgotten its insulting
echo.

Nevertheless, there are fine things in Guarini, and
such as the world has consented to remember, though
not of this all-affecting sort. One of these is the
address to the woods, beginning—

Care selve beate,
E voi, solinghi e taciturni orrori,
Di riposo e di pace alberghi veri :—

an exordium, which somebody (was it Mrs. Katherine
Phillips, the "matchless Orinda "?) has well translated :—

Dear happy groves, and you, the dark retreat
Of silent horror, rest's eternal seat.

We are sorry we cannot recollect any more. It expresses
the wish, which so many have felt, to live in retirement,
and be devoted to the beauties of nature. Another
passage, more generally known, turns also upon a very
general feeling of regret—that of seeing spring-time
reappear, unaccompanied with the joys we have lost.
Guarini was safer in following his original into these
sincere corners of the heart, than when he attempted to
refute him with a boy's copy-book. The passage is very
beautiful, and no less popular :—

O Primavera, gioventù de l' anno,
Bella madre de' fiori,
D' erbe novelle e di novelli amori,
Tu torni ben ; ma teco
Non tornano i sereni
E fortunati dì de le mie gioje :
Tu torni ben, tu torni,
Ma teco altro non torna
Che del perduto mio caro tesoro
La rimembranza misera e dolente :

Tu quella sei, tu quella,
Ch' era pur dianzi si vezzosa e bella ;
Ma non son io già quel ch'un tempo fui,
Si caro a gli occhi altrui.

Pastor Fido, atto iii. sc. i.

O Spring, thou youthful beauty of the year,
Mother of flowers, bringer of warbling quires,
Of all sweet new green things and new desires,
Thou, Spring, returnest ; but, alas ! with thee
No more return to me
The calm and happy days these eyes were used to see.
Thou, thou returnest, thou,
But with thee returns now
Nought else but dread remembrance of the pleasure
I took in my lost treasure.
Thou still, thou still, art the same blithe, sweet thing
Thou ever wast, O Spring ;
But I, in whose weak orbs these tears arise,
Am what I was no more, dear to another's eyes.

The repetitions in this beautiful lament,

Tu torni ben, tu torni, &c.,

are particularly affecting. Perhaps the tone of them
was caught from Ariosto :—

Non son, non sono io quel che paio in viso :
Quel ch'era Orlando, è morto, ed è sotterra.

Furioso, canto xxiii. st. 128.

No more, no more am I what I appear :
He that Orlando was, is dead and gone.

It is no critical violence at any time to pass from the Italian schools of poetry to those of our own country. They have always been closely connected, at least on the side of England, for the others knew little of their Northern admirers—men in whom Ariosto and Tasso would have delighted. Our language, till of late years, was not so widely spread as the Italian.

Our earliest pastoral poet of any name is Spenser; and a great name he is, though he was not a great pastoral poet. He was deeply intimate both with Greek and Italian pastoral; but in admiring Theocritus, and hoping to rival his natural language, he unwisely attempted to engraft the sweet fruit of the south on the rudest crab-apple of northern rusticity. Hence, in his only pastoral professing to be such, entitled the *Shepherd's Calendar*, he has almost entirely failed. There are some touching lines in the story of the *Fox and Kid*, and a beautiful paraphrase of that of *Cupid and the Fowler*, from Bion; but in truth, with all his love of the woods and fields, for which he had a poet's passion, and never could be without, Spenser was not qualified to excel as a purely pastoral writer. He was too learned for it, too full of the writers before him, and could not dispense with their chivalry and mythology. His words were Greek rather than English;

9

or if English, they were the English of a former time.
When Venus and the Graces were not there, he saw
enchantresses and knights-errant. He always had
visions, as Milton had, either of Jove or Proserpine,
or of

> Faery damsels met in forests wide
> By knights of Logres and of Lyones,
> Lancelot, or Pelleas, or Pellenore.

But this elevated him to the high ideal of the
subject; and no man could have written so fine a
pastoral as he, of the classical or romantic sort, had he
set his luxuriant wits to it, instead of attempting to get
up an uncouth dance with the "clouted shoon" of
Hobbinol and Davie. He could have beaten Ben
Jonson, Fletcher, and all. Under picturesque influ-
ences, he never failed to add beauty to beauty. In the
original of the passage we have alluded to, which he
imitated from Bion, (the story of *Cupid and the
Fowler*,) Bion merely makes the young fowler take
Cupid in the trees for a bird, and endeavour to ensnare
him; ending with a pretty admonition, from an old
master of the craft, not to persevere in his attempt,
seeing that the bird in question was a very dangerous
bird, and would come to him soon enough by-and-by of
his own accord. In Spenser, Cupid has wings coloured
like a peacock's train; and after flashing out beautifully

from the bushes to a tree, the little god leaps from bough to bough, and playfully catches the stones thrown at him in his hand. All the introductory details, too, which are full of truth, are Spenser's :—

At length within the yvie todde
(There shrowded was the little god)
   I heard a busie bustling ;
I bent my bolt against the bush,
Listning if anie thing did rush,
   But then heard no more rustling.
Tho, peeping close into the thicke,
Might see the moving of some quicke,
   Whose shape appearèd not ;
But were it faerie, feend, or snake,
My courage yearn'd it to awake,
   And manfully thereat shotte :
With that sprang forth a naked swayne,
With spotted winges like peacock's trayne,
   And, laughing, lope to a tree ;
His gylden quiver at his back ;
And silver bowe, which was but slacke,
   Which lightly he bent at me :
That seeing, I leveld againe,
And shot at him with might and mayne,
   As thick as it had hayled :
So long I shott, that all was spent ;
The pumie-stones I hastily hent,
   And threw ; but nought avayled :
He was so nimble and so wight,
From bough to bough he leppèd light,
   And oft the pumies latchèd.

       —*Shepherd's Calendar*, March, v. 67.

Latched, is *caught;* and *pumies*, and *pumie-stones*,
are *pumice*-stones, a very light mineral.   The fowler is
considerate, and would not break the bird's head.   This
passage is one of the least obsolete in its style of all the
Shepherd's Calendar; yet what a pity to see it deformed
with words requiring explanation, such as *latched* for
caught, tho for *then, lope* for *leaped*, &c.   With the like
needless perversity, forgetful of his elevated calling,
Spenser, in his pastoral character, delights to designate
himself as " Colin Clout," as though he were nothing
better than a patch in the very heels of clodhopping.
And yet, under this name, he sees the Nymphs and
Graces dancing round his shepherdess upon Mount
Acidale !   The passage, otherwise, is one of his most
elegant pieces of invention ; and with the Grecian
topography, may be said to exhibit the very highest
region and crown of the pastoral side of Parnassus.
Sir Calidore, the Knight of Courtesy (for thus does he
mix up the classical and romantic grounds ; but no
matter for that, since they are both in the regions of
imagination), hears a noise of music and dancing as he
is approaching the top of Mount Acidale. Upon looking
amongst the trees, when he reaches it, he sees a shepherd piping to his love, in the midst of

An hundred naked maidens, lily-white,
All rangèd in a ring, and dancing in delight.

But we must not lose the description of the place
itself :—

It was an hill, plaiste in an open plaine,
That round about is border'd with a wood
Of matchless hight, that seem'd th' earth to disdaine,
In which all trees of honour stately stood,
And did all winter as in summer bud,
Spredding pavillions for the birds to bowre,
Which in their lower braunches sang aloud ;
And in their tops the soring hawk did towre,
Sitting like king of foules in majesty and powre :

And at the foote thereof a gentle flud
His silver waves did softly tumble down,
Unmar'd with ragged mosse or filthy mud ;
Ne mote wild beastes, ne mote the ruder clowne,
Thereto approach ; ne filth mote therein drowne :
But Nymphs and Faeries by the bancks did sit
In the wood's shade, which did the waters crowne,
Keeping all noysome things away from it,
And to the water's fall tuning their accents fit.

And on the top thereof a spacious plaine
Did spred itselfe, to serve to all delight,
Either to daunce, when they to daunce would faine
Or else to course about their bases light ;
Ne ought there wanted, which for pleasure might
Desirèd be, or thence to banish bale ;
So pleasantly the hill with equall hight
Did seem to overlooke the lowly vale ;
Therefore it rightly cleepèd was Mount Acidale.*

* Perhaps from a Greek root, expressing carelessness or quiet.

They say that Venus, when she did dispose
Herselfe to pleasaunce, usèd to resort
Unto this place, and therein to repose
And rest herself, as in a gladsome port;
Or with the Graces, there to play and sport;
That even her own Cytheron, though in it
She usèd most to keep her royall court,
And in her soveraine majesty to sit,
She, in regard thereof, refusde and thought unfit.

Unto this place when as the elfin knight
Approacht, him seemèd that the merry sound
Of a shrill pipe he playing heard on hight,
And many feete fast thumping th' hollow ground,
That through the woods their echo did rebound.
He hither drew, to weete what mote it be:
There he a troupe of ladies dauncing found
Full merrily, and making gladfull glee,
And in the midst a shepherd piping he did see.

He durst not enter into th' open greene,
For dread of them unawares to be descryde,
For breaking of their daunce, if he were seene;
But in the covert of the wood did byde,
Beholding all, yet of them unespyde:
There he did see, that pleased much his sight,
That even he himself his eyes envyde,
An hundred naked maidens, lilly white,
All raungèd in a ring and dauncing in delight.

In the middle of this orb of fair creatures, the
beauty of which there is nothing of the sort to equal,
(unless it be those circles of lily-white stamens which,
with such exquisite mystery, adorn the commonest

flower-cups—so profuse of her poetry is Nature !), Sir
Calidore sees "three other ladies," both dancing and
singing—to wit, the Graces; and in the midst of
"those same three" was yet another lady, or rather
"damsel" (for she was of rustic origin), crowned with
a garland of roses, and so beautiful, that she was the
very gem of the ring, and "graced" the Graces themselves. The hundred nymphs, as they danced, threw
flowers upon her; the Graces endowed her with the
gifts which she reflected upon them, enhanced; and a
shepherd sat piping to them all.

Never, surely, was such deification of a "country
lass;" and well might the poet hail his spectacle in a
rapture of self-complacency, and encourage his pipe to
play on : —

> *Pype, jolly shepheard ! pype thou now apace*
> *Unto thy love, that made thee low to lout.*

(He has raised her from the condition to which he
stooped to obtain her.)

Thy love is present there with thee in place—

(That is, in the midst of his poetry and his
fame.)

Thy love is there advaunst *to be another Grace.*

But a mishap is on the heels of this vision, con-

nected with our author's professed attempts at pastoral;
for so we have little doubt it is, though the commentators have given it another meaning. Sir Calidore,
envying his eyes a sight which so " enriched" them,
left the covert through which he looked, and went
towards it :—

> But soone as he appearèd to their view,
> They vanisht all away, out of his sight,
> And cleane were gone, which way he never knew,
> All save the shepherd ; who, for fell despight
> Of that displeasure, broke his bag-pipe quight,
> And made great mone for that unhappy turne ;
> But Calidore, though no less sorry wight
> For that mishap, yet seeing him to mourne,
> Drew neare, that he the truth of all by him might learne.

Sir Calidore, the Knight of Courtesy, is understood
to be Sir Philip Sidney, who, in his *Defence of Poesy*, had
objected to the style of the *Shepherd's Calendar ;* and
as his word was taken for law in matters of taste, and
the criticism was probably fatal to the poet's continuance
in that style (for at all events he dropped it), we have
scarcely a doubt that Spenser alludes to the fact of his
giving up pastoral writing in consequence. He breaks
his pipe ; not, it seems (like most authors, when they
give way to critics), without much secret vexation—nay,
" a fell despight," as he calls it ; candidly, if not a little
maliciously, owning the whole extent of his feelings on

the subject to his illustrious critic, who had since become his friend. It was a disadvantage which his pride could not feel itself easy with, till it had set it to rights. The following is the passage in Sidney's essay :—

The *Shepherd's Kalander* hath much poetry in his eclogues, indeed worthy the reading, if I be not deceived. That same framing of his style to an old rustic language, I dare not allow; since neither Theocritus in Greek, Virgil in Latin, nor Sannazarro in Italian, did affect it.

He means that Theocritus and the others wrote in the language of their times, and that to be obsolete is not to be natural. Spenser, it is to be observed, expressly designates himself in this episode as Colin Clout, which is the title he assumed as the author of the *Shepherd's Calendar;* a "country lassie" is his goddess in that work ; and it seems far more likely that under this identity of appellation he should complain, in one poem, of the discouragement given to another, than simply shadow forth (as the commentators think) the circumstance of Sir Philip Sidney's having drawn him from the country to the court. In what consisted the abrupt intervention of a proceeding like that ? What particular vision did it dissipate ? Or how could he pretend any right of soreness in his tone of complaint about it ? And he is very sore indeed at the knight's

interruption, notwithstanding his courtesy. Tell me,
says Calidore—

> Tell me what mote these dainty damsels be,
> Which here with thee do make their pleasant playes :
> Right happy thou, that mayst them freely see ;
> But why, when I them saw, fled they away from me ?
>
> *Not I so happy*, answered then that swaine,
> *As thou unhappy*, which them thence did chase,
> Whom by no meanes thou canst recall againe.

He could not look back with comfort upon having been
forced to give up his pastoral visions.

But to return to our subject. The all-including
genius of Shakspeare has given the finest intimations
of pastoral writing in some of the masques introduced
in his plays, and in his plays themselves; if indeed
As You Like It might not equally as well be called a
pastoral play as a comedy; though, to be sure, the
duke and his followers do not willingly take to the
woods, with the exception of the "sad shepherd"
Jacques ; and this is a great drawback on the pleasures
of the occasion, which ought to breathe as freely as the
air and the wild roses. Rosalind, however, is a very bud
of the pastoral ideal, peeping out of her forest jerkin.
Again, in the *Winter's Tale*, where the good housewife
is recorded, who has "her face o' fire" with attending
to the guests, and "my sister," who has the purchase

of the eatables, " lays it on " (as her brother the clown
says) in the article of rice, there is the truest pastoral
of both kinds, the ideal and the homely :—

SHEPHERD. Fie, daughter ! When my old wife liv'd, upon
This day she was both pantler, butler, cook,—
Both dame and servant ; *welcom'd all, serv'd all ;*
Would sing her song, and dance her turn ; now here,
At upper end o' the table, now i' the middle ;
On his shoulder, and his ; her face o' fire
With labour ; and the thing she took to quench it,
She would to each one sip.

What a poet, and what a painter ! Now a Raphael,
or Michael Angelo ; now a Jan Steen or a Teniers.
Here also is Autolycus, the most exquisite of impudent
vagabonds, better even than the *Brass* of Sir John
Vanbrugh ; selling his love ballads, so without inde-
cency, "which is strange," and another ballad of a
singing *Fish*, with " five justices' hands to it," to vouch
for its veracity. But, above all, here is Perdita :—

The prettiest low-born lass that ever
Ran on the green sward.

No shepherdess, but Flora,
Peering in April's front.

Perdita, also, though supposed to be a shepherdess
born, is a *Sicilian* princess, and makes our BLUE JAR
glisten again in the midst of its native sun and flowers.

O Prosèrpina !
For the flowers now that, frighted, thou let'st fall
From Dis's waggon !—

("Waggon," be it observed, was as much a word of
respect in those days as "chariot" is now.)

Daffodils
That come before the swallow dares, *and take*
The winds of March with beauty ; violets, dim,
But sweeter than the lids of Juno's eyes,
Or Cytherea's breath ;
bold oxlips, and
The crown-imperial ; lilies of all kinds,
The flower-de-luce being one. O, these I lack
To make you garlands of ; and, my sweet friend,
[*Turning to her lover.*
To strew him o'er and o'er.
FLORIZEL.   What ! like a corse ?
PERDITA. No : like a bank, for love to lie and play on.
Not like a corse ; or if,—not to be buried,
But quick, and in mine arms.

Shelley has called a woman "one of Shakspeare's
women," implying by that designation all that can be
suggested of grace and sweetness.   They were "very
subtle," as Mr. Wordsworth said of the French ladies.
Not that they were French ladies, or English either ;
but Nature's and refinement's best possible gentle-
women all over the world. Tullia d'Aragona, the Italian
poetess, who made all her suitors love one another instead of quarrel, must have been a Shakspeare woman.

Gaspara Stampa was another ; and we should take the authoress of *Auld Robin Gray* for one.

Sidney's sister, Pembroke's mother,

and Lucy, Countess of Bedford, must have been such. So was Mrs. Brooke, who wrote *Emily Montague ;* and probably Madame Riccoboni; and certainly my Lady Winchelsea, who worshipped friendship, and green retreats, and her husband ;—terrible people all, to look upon, if the very sweetness of their virtue did not enable us to bear it.

Ben Jonson left an unfinished dramatic pastoral, entitled the *Sad Shepherd.* It is a story of Robin Hood, in connection with a shepherd who has gone melancholy mad for the supposed death of his mistress —a lucky character for the exalted wilfulness of the author's style. The lover opens the play with the following elegant extravagance :—

ÆGLAMOUR. Here she was wont to go ! and here ! and
  here !
Just where those daisies, pinks, and violets grow :
The world may find the spring by following her.

This is a truly lover-like fancy ; and the various, impulsive, and flowery versification is perfect. Ben Jonson can never leave out his learning. The lost mistress must be compared, in the impossible lightness of her

step, with Virgil's Camilla, who ran over the tops of
corn :—

> For other print her airy steps ne'er left ;
> Her treading would not bend a blade of grass,
> Or shake the downy blow-ball from his stalk.

What unsubstantial womanhood !   How different from
the bride of Bedreddin Hassan !

> " Up, up in haste ! " the young man cries :
> Ah ! slender waist ! she cannot rise
> For heavy hips, that say, " Sit still,"
> And make her linger 'gainst her will.
>
> —TORRENS's *Arabian Nights.*

The best passage in the *Sad Shepherd* is a description
of a witch and her habits—a subject which every way
suited the arbitrary and sullen side of the poet's notions
of power.   It also enabled him to show his reading, as
he takes care to let us know, by means of one of the
bystanders :—

> ALKEN.   Know ye the witch's dell ?
> SCATHLOCK. No more than I do know the ways of hell.
> ALKEN. Within a gloomy dimble she doth dwell,
> Down in a pit, o'ergrown with brakes and briers,
> *Close by the ruins of a shaken abbey,*
> *Torn with an earthquake down unto the ground,*
> *'Mongst graves and grots, near an old charnel-house,*
> Where you shall find her sitting in her form,
> As fearful and melancholic as that
> She is about with caterpillars' kells
> And knotty cobwebs, rounded in with spells.

Thence she steals forth to revel in the fogs
And *rotten mists* upon the fens and bogs,
Down to the drownèd lands of Lincolnshire ;
To make ewes cast their lambs, swine eat their farrow,
The housewife's tun not work, nor the milk churn !
Writhe children's wrists, and suck their breath in sleep,
Get vials of their blood ; and where the sea
Casts up its slimy ooze, search for a weed
To open locks with, and to rivet charms,
Planted about her in the wicked feat
Of all her mischiefs, which are manifold.

    JOHN. I wonder such a story could be told
Of her dire deeds.

    GEORGE.   I thought a witch's banks
Had enclosed nothing but the merry pranks
Of some old woman.

    SCARLET.   Yes, her malice more.

    SCATHLOCK. As it would quickly appear had we the store
Of his collects.

    GEORGE.   Ay, this good learned man
Can speak her rightly.

    SCARLET.   He knows her shifts and haunts.

    ALKEN. And all her wiles and turns. The venom'd plants
Wherewith she kills ; where the sad mandrake grows,
Whose groans are dreadful ; the dead-numbing nightshade,
The stupifying hemlock, adder's tongue,
And martagan ; the shrieks of luckless owls
We hear, and croaking night-crows in the air ;
Green-bellied snakes, blue fire-drakes in the sky,
And giddy flitter-mice with leather wings,
And scaly beetles *with their habergeons,*
That make a humming murmur as they fly.
There, in the stocks of trees, *white faies do dwell,*
And span-long elves that dance about a pool
With each a little changeling in their arms !

> And airy spirits play with falling stars,
> And mount the sphere of fire to kiss the moon,
> While she sits reading (by the glow-worm's light,
> Of rotten wood, *o'er which the worm hath crept*)
> The baneful schedule of her nocent charms.

The idea of "span-long elves" who dance about a pool, carrying each a stolen infant, that must be bigger than themselves, is a very capital and fantastic horror.

Old burly and strong-sensation-loving Ben (as his friend Chapman, or Mr. Bentham, might have called him) could show, however, a great deal of delicacy when he had a mind to it.   He could turn his bluster into a zephyr that inspired the young genius of Milton. Some of his court masques are pastoral; and the following is the style in which he receives the king and queen. Maia (the goddess of May) says—

> If all the pleasures were distill'd
> Of *every* flower in *every* field—

(This kind of return of words was not common then, as he has since made it)

> And all that Hybla's hives do yield,
> Were into one broad mazer fill'd;
> If thereto added all the gums
> And spice that from Panchaia comes,
> The odours that Hydaspes lends,
> Or Phœnix proves before she ends;
> If all the air my Flora drew,
> Or spirit that Zephyr ever blew,

Were put therein ; *and all the dew*
That ever rosy morning knew ;
Yet all, diffused upon this bower,
To make one sweet detaining hour,
Were much too little for the grace
And honour you vouchsafe the place.

In the masque of *Oberon*, Silenus bids his Satyrs rouse up a couple of sleeping Sylvans, who ought to have been keeping watch ; "at which," says the poet's direction, "the Satyrs fell suddenly into this catch"— Musicians know it well :—

> *Buz*, quoth the blue fly ;
> *Hum*, quoth the bee ;
> *Buz and hum they cry,*
> *And so do we.*
> In his *ear*, in his *nose,*
> *Thus*, do you see !   [*They tickle them.*
> He eat *the dormouse,*
> Else it was *he.*

It is impossible that anything could better express than this, either the wild and practical joking of the Satyrs, or the action of the thing described, or the quaintness and fitness of the images, or the melody and even the harmony, the *intercourse*, of the musical words, one with another. None but a boon companion with a very musical ear could have written it. It was not for nothing that Ben lived in the time of the fine old English composers, Bull and Ford ; or partook his canary with his "lov'd Alphonso," as he calls him,—the Signor Ferrabosco.

We have not yet done with this delightful portion of our subject. Fletcher and Milton await us still; together with the pastoral poet, William Browne; and a few other poets, who, though they wrote no pastorals, were pastoral men.

CHAPTER VIII.

ENGLISH PASTORAL—(Continued); AND SCOTCH PASTORAL.

FLETCHER'S " FAITHFUL SHEPHERDESS." — PROBABLE
REASON OF ITS NON-SUCCESS.—" COMUS " AND " LYCIDAS.'
—DR. JOHNSON'S " WORLD."—BURNS AND ALLAN RAMSAY.

H E title and story of the
Sad Shepherd of Ben
Jonson, in combination
with those of the *Faith-
ful Shepherd* (*Pastor Fido*)
of Guarini, appear to have
suggested to Fletcher his
Faithful Shepherdess. This
is undoubtedly the chief pastoral play in our language,
though, with all its beauties, we can hardly think it

10—2

ought to have been such, considering what Shakspeare and Spenser have shown that they could have
done in this Arcadian region. The illustrious author,
exquisite poet as he was, and son of a bishop to boot,
had the misfortune, with his friend Beaumont, to be
what is called a " man upon town ; " which polluted his
sense of enjoyment and rendered him but imperfectly
in earnest, even when he most wished to be so.
Hence his subserviency to the taste of those painful
gentlemen called men of pleasure, and his piecing out
his better sentiments with exaggeration. Hence the
revolting character, in this play, of a "Wanton
Shepherdess," which is an offence to the very
voluptuousness it secretly intended to interest; and
hence the opposite offence of the character of the
" Faithful Shepherdess " herself, who is ostentatiously
made such a paragon of chastity, and values herself so
excessively on the self-denial, that the virtue itself is
compromised, and you can see that the author had very
little faith in it. And we have little doubt that this was
the cause why the play was damned (for such is the
startling fact), and not the ignorance of the audience, to
which Beaumont and Ben Jonson indignantly attributed
it. The audience could not reconcile such painful,
and, as it must have appeared to them, such hypocritical
contradictions: and very distressing to the author must

it have been to find, that he had himself contributed to create that sceptical tone of mind in the public respecting both himself and the female sex, which refused to take him at his word when he was for putting on a graver face, and claiming their ultra-belief in all that he chose to assume. The "Faithful Shepherdess" is a young widow, who is always talking of devoting herself to her husband's memory; and her lover Thenot is so *passionately* enamoured of her, that he says if she were to give up the devotion, his passion would be lost. He *entreats* her at once to "hear him" and to "*deny!*" This child's play is what the audience could not tolerate. It was a pity; for there are passages in the *Faithful Shepherdess* as lovely as poet could write. We are never tired of hearing—

> How the pale Phœbe, hunting in a grove,
> First saw the boy Endymion, from whose eyes
> She took eternal fire that never dies;
> *How she convey'd him softly in a sleep,*
> *His temples bound with poppy, to the steep*
> *Head of old Latmos, where she stoops each night,*
> *Gilding the mountain with her brother's light,*
> *To kiss her sweetest.*

So of the dessert gathered by the Satyr for the nymph Syrinx :—

> Here be grapes, whose lusty blood
> Is the learned poet's good;

Sweeter yet did never crown
The head of Bacchus; nuts more brown
Than the squirrel's teeth that crack them :.
Deign, oh, fairest fair, to take them.
For these black-eyed Driope
Hath oftentimes commanded me
With my claspèd knee to climb :
See how well *the lusty time*
Hath decked their rising cheeks in red,
Such as on your lips is spread.
Here be berries for a queen,
Some be red, some be green ;
These are of that luscious meat,
The great god Pan himself doth eat ;
All these, and what the woods can yield,
The hanging mountain or the field,
I freely offer, and ere long
Will bring you more, more sweet and strong ;
Till then humbly leave I take,
Lest the great Pan do awake,
That sleeping lies in a deep glade
Under a broad beech's shade.
I must go, I must run,
Swifter than the fiery sun.

See also the love made by the river-god at the end of
the third Act, which we have not room to quote ; and
the Satyr's account of dawn, which opens with the four
most exquisite lines perhaps in the whole play :—

See, the day begins to break,
And the light shoots like a streak
Of subtle fire.—The wind blows cold,
While the morning doth unfold.

Who has not felt this mingled charmingness and chilliness (we do not use the words for the sake of the alliteration) at the first opening of the morning! Yet none but the finest poets venture upon thus combining pleasure with something that might be thought a drawback. But it is truth; and it is truth in which the beauty surmounts the pain; and therefore they give it. And how simple and straightforward is every word! There are no artificial tricks of composition here. The words are not suggested to the truth by the author, but to the author by the truth. We feel the wind blowing as simply as it does in nature; so that if the reader be artificially trained, and does not bring a feeling for truth with him analogous to that of the poet, the very simplicity is in danger of losing him the perception of the beauty. And yet there is art as well as nature in the verses; for art in the poet must perfect what nature does by her own art. Observe, for instance, the sudden and strong emphasis on the word *shoots*, and the variety of tone and modulation in the whole passage, with the judicious exceptions of the two *o*'s in the " wind blows cold," which have the solemn continuous sound of what it describes: also, the corresponding ones in " doth unfold," which maintain the like continuity of the growing daylight. And exquisite, surely, is the dilatory and golden sound of the word "morning" between them :

> The wind blows cold,
> While the *mor*-ning doth unfold.

Milton's *Comus*, though not equal throughout to the *Faithful Shepherdess* in descriptive judgment (for it talks of " groves of myrrh and cinnamon " on the banks of a British river), is altogether a finer poem, and a far better recommendation of chastity. Indeed, it might rather have been called *Castitas* than *Comus;* for *Comus* has little justice done to his powers of temptation. Perhaps Fletcher's failure in recommending chastity suggested the hope of surpassing him to Milton. His emulation of particular passages in the *Faithful Shepherdess*, particularly on that subject, has been noticed by the commentators. But *Comus* is a mask, not a pastoral. It can hardly even be called a pastoral mask ; for the shepherd is the least person in it ; and though the Italians identify the pastoral with the sylvan drama, or fable transacted in the woods, which are the scene of action in *Comus*, the reader feels that the woods have really almost as little to do with it as the fields ;—that the moral, in fact, is all in all ; which is the reason why nobody takes very heartily to the subject, especially as Milton acts in morals like a kind of solemn partisan, and does not run, like

Shakspeare, the whole circle of humanity in arguing his question.

Milton's only real pastoral (with the exception of the country part of the *Allegro*) is his allegorical monody on the death of his friend King,—the *Lycidas;* and a beautiful one it is, though Dr. Johnson, in his one-sided misapplication of a right principle, laughed at grief which departs from the ordinary phases of life, and which talks of nymphs and river-gods, and " satyrs with cloven heel." " Grief," he said, " does not talk of such things;" to which Warton said very truly, "But Poetry does;" and he might have added (still more literally than he puts it), that Grief does so too, when it is the grief of one young poet mourning for another. Johnson says that Milton and his friend were not "nursed on the same hill," as represented in *Lycidas;* and that they did not "feed the same flock," &c. But they were, and they did. They were nursed on the same hill of Arcady, and fed the same flock of the ideal pastoral life ; and very grievous it was for them to be torn asunder, to be deprived by death of their mutual delight in Theocritus, and Virgil, and Spenser, the beloved haunts of their minds, things which it has agonized friends and poets to be torn away from, both before and since the time of Milton, however little they may have been cared for by dear, good, dictatorial, purblind, un-ideal Dr. Johnson, whose world, though it was a wit's and a sage's world too, was not the universal and still sager world of the poet, but made up (exclusively) of the Strand, hypochondria, charity, bigotry, wit, argument, and a good dinner;—a pretty region, but not the green as *well* as smoky world of Nature and Shakspeare.

Fault has been found also with the intermixture of theology in *Lycidas;* but it is to be defended on the same ground—namely, that Milton's young friend studied theology with him as well as poetry; and hence the propriety of introducing the pilot of the Galilean lake.

One ought to be grateful for it, if only for its giving the poet occasion to dismiss the solemn vision, and encourage, in those lovely verses, the beautiful fictions of Paganism and Theocritus to come back :—

> Return, Alphéus ; the dread voice is past
> That shrunk thy streams ; return, *Sicilian Muse,*
> And call the vales, and bid them hither cast
> Their bells and flowerets of a thousand hues.
> *Ye valleys low, where the mild whispers use*
> *Of shades, and wanton winds, and gushing brooks,*
> On whose fresh lap the swart-star sparely looks,
> Throw hither all your quaint-enamell'd eyes
> That on the green turf *suck the honied showers,*
> And purple all the ground with vernal flowers.
> Bring the rathe primrose that forsaken dies,

The tufted crow-toe, and pale jessamine,
The white pink, and the pansy, *freak'd* with jet,
The glowing violet,
The musk-rose, and the well-attired woodbine,
With cowslips wan, that hang the pensive head,
And every flower that sad embroidery wears ;
Bid amaranthus all his beauty shed,
And daffodillies fill their cups with tears,
To strew the laureat herse where Lycid lies.

*   *   *   *   *

Thus sang the swain to the oaks and rills,
While the still morn went out with sandals grey.

These are the chief pastoral writers in the language
of the ideal class. Pope professed to be a classical
pastoral writer, and split, accordingly, on the hard rock
of Latin imitation. Even Gay's burlesque pastoral was
better, for it went to the real fields for its imagery ; and
Phillips would have surpassed both, if he had not been
affected. His verses from Copenhagen, describing a
northern winter, are fresh from Nature.

Allan Ramsay is the prince of the homely pastoral
drama. Burns wrote in this class of poetry at no such
length as Ramsay ; but he was pastoral poetry itself, in
the shape of an actual, glorious peasant, vigorous as if
Homer had written him, and tender as generous
strength, or as memories of the grave. Ramsay and he
have helped Scotland for ever to take pride in its
heather, and its braes, and its bonny rivers, and be

ashamed of no beauty or honest truth, in high estate or
in low;—an incalculable blessing. Ramsay, to be sure,
with all his genius, and though he wrote an entire and
excellent dramatic pastoral, in five legitimate acts, is
but a small part of Burns;—is but a field in a corner
compared with the whole Scots pastoral region. He has
none of Burns's pathos; none of his grandeur; none of
his burning energy; none of his craving after universal
good.   How universal is Burns!   What mirth in his
cups!   What softness in his tears!   What sympathy in
his very satire!   What manhood in everything!   If
Theocritus, the inventor of a loving and affecting Polyphemus, could have foreseen the verses on the *Mouse*
and the *Daisy* turned up with plough, the *Tam o'
Shanter*, *O Willie brew'd a peck o' maut*, *Ye banks
and braes o' bonnie Doon*, &c., (not to mention a
hundred others, which have less to do with our subject,)
tears of admiration would have rushed into his eyes.

Nevertheless Allan Ramsay is not only entitled to
the designation we have given him, but in some respects
is the best pastoral writer in the world.   There are, in
truth, two sorts of genuine pastoral—the high ideal of
Fletcher and Milton, which is justly to be considered
the more poetical,—and the homely ideal, as set forth
by Allan Ramsay and some of the Idyls of Theocritus, and which gives us such feelings of nature

and passion as poetical rustics not only can, but have entertained, and eloquently described. And we think the *Gentle Shepherd*, "in some respects," the best pastoral that ever was written, not because it has anything, in a poetical point of view, to compare with Fletcher and Milton, but because there is, upon the whole, more faith and more love in it, and because the kind of idealized truth which it undertakes to represent, is delivered in a more corresponding and satisfactory form than in any other entire pastoral drama. In fact, the *Gentle Shepherd* has no alloy whatsoever to its pretensions, *such as they are*—no failure in plot, language, or character—nothing answering to the coldness and irrelevances of *Comus*, nor to the offensive and untrue violations of decorum in the "Wanton Shepherdess" of Fletcher's pastoral, and the pedantic and ostentatious chastity of his Faithful one. It is a pure, healthy, natural, and (of its kind) perfect plant, sprung out of an unluxuriant but not ungenial soil; not hung with the beauty and fragrance of the productions of the higher regions of Parnassus; not waited upon by spirits and enchanted music; a dog-rose, if you will; say rather, a rose in a cottage-garden, dabbled with the morning dew, and plucked by an honest lover to give to his mistress.

Allan Ramsay's poem is not only a probable and

pleasing story, containing charming pictures, much
knowledge of life, and a good deal of quiet humour, but
in some respects it may be called classical, if by
classical is meant ease, precision, and unsuperfluousness
of style. Ramsay's diction is singularly straightforward,
seldom needing the assistance of inversions; and he
rarely says anything for the purpose of " filling up ; "—
two freedoms from defect the reverse of vulgar and
commonplace ; nay, the reverse of a great deal of what
pretends to be fine writing, and is received as such. We
confess we never tire of dipping into it, " on and off,"
any more than into Fletcher, or Milton, or into
Theocritus himself, who, for the union of something
higher with true pastoral, is unrivalled in short pieces.
The *Gentle Shepherd* is not a forest, nor a mountain-
side, nor Arcady ; but it is a field full of daisies, with a
brook in it, and a cottage " at the sunny end ; " and
this we take to be no mean thing, either in the real or
the ideal world. Our Jar of Honey may well lie for a
few moments among its heather, albeit filled from
Hybla. There are bees, " look you," in Habbie's How.
Theocritus and Allan shake hands over a shepherd's
pipe. Take the beginning of Scene ii. Act i., both for
description and dialogue :—

A flowrie howm between twa verdant braes,
Where lassies use to wash and spread their claes ;

A trottin' birnie wimplin' through the ground,
Its channel pebbles shining smooth and round.
Here view *twa barefoot beauties,* clean and clear,
First please your eye, next gratify your ear,
While Jenny *what she wishes discommends,*
And Meg, with better sense, true love defends.

JENNY. Come, Meg, lets fa' to work upon this green,
This shining day will bleach our linen clean :
The waters clear, the lift unclouded blue,
Will make them *like a lily wet wi' dew.*

PEGGY. Gae far'er up the burn to Habbie's How,
Where a' the sweets o' spring and simmer grow ;
There 'tween twa birks, out ower a little lin,
The water fa's, and maks a singin' din ;
A pool breast-deep, beneath as clear as glass,
Kisses, wi' easy whirls, the bordering grass.
We'll end our washing while the morning's cool,
And when the day grows het, we'll to the pool,
There wash oursells ; 't is healthfu' now in May,
And sweetly cauler on sae warm a day.

This is an out-door picture. Here is an indoor one
quite as good—nay, better :—

While Peggy laces up her bosom fair,
With a blue snood Jenny binds up her hair ;
Glaud by his morning ingle takes a beek ;
The rising sun shines motty through the reek ;
A pipe his mouth, the lasses please his een,
And now and then his joke maun intervene.

We would quote, if we could—only it might not look
so proper, when isolated—the whole song at the close of

Act the Second. The first line of it alone is worth all
Pope's pastorals put together, and (we were going to
add) half of those of Virgil ; but we reverence too much
the great follower of the Greeks, and true lover of the
country. There is more sentiment, and equal nature, in
the song at the end of Act the Fourth. Peggy is taking
leave of her lover, who is going abroad :—

> At setting day and rising morn,
>   Wi' saul that still shall love thee,
> I'll ask o' Heaven thy safe return,
>   Wi' a' that can improve thee.
> I'll visit aft the birkin bush,
>   Where first thou kindly tauld me
> Sweet tales of love, *and hid my blush,*
>   *Whilst round thou didst infald me.*
>
> To a' our haunts I will repair,
>   To greenwood, shaw, or fountain ;
> Or where the summer day I'd share
>   Wi' thee upon yon mountain.
> There will I tell the trees and flowers
>   Frae thoughts unfeign'd and tender,
> *By vows* you're mine, *by love* is yours
>   A heart that cannot wander.

The charming and (so to speak) natural flattery of
the loving delicacy of this distinction—

> *By vows* you're mine, *by love* is yours,

was never surpassed by a passion the most refined. It
reminds us of a like passage in the anonymous words

(Shakspeare might have written them) of the fine old English madrigal by Ford, "Since first I saw your face." Perhaps Ford himself wrote them; for the author of that music had sentiment enough in him for anything. The passage we allude to is—

> What, I that *loved*, and you that *liked*,
> Shall *we* begin to wrangle?

The highest refinement of the heart, though too rare in most classes, is luckily to be found in all; and hence it is, that certain meetings of extremes in lovers of different ranks in life are not always to be attributed either to a failure of taste on the one side, or unsuitable pretensions on the other. Scottish dukes have been known to meet with real Gentle-Shepherd heroines; and everybody knows the story of a lowly Countess of Exeter, who was too sensitive to survive the disclosure of the rank to which her lover had raised her.

CHAPTER IX.

ENGLISH PASTORAL.—(Concluded.)

PASTORALS OF WILLIAM BROWNE.—PASTORAL MEN :—CER-
VANTES—BOCCACCIO—CHAUCER—COWLEY—THOMSON—
SHENSTONE, ETC.

ONLY undramatic pastorals in the language worth mention are those of Browne, a young poet, who wrote in the beginning of the reign of James the First. He won the praises of Drayton and Ben Jonson, and may remind the reader of some of the earlier poems of Keats. He was a real poet, with a great love of external nature, and much delicacy and generosity of sentiment; and had his judgment been matured, would now have been as much admired by the many as he is regarded by the few. His verses are of such unequal merit, that it is difficult to select any long passage, or scarcely, indeed, any short one, that does not contain matter unworthy of him; yet in all may be discerned promise, in many sweetness and beauty, in some grandeur; and there is nobody who loves poets of the Spenser school, but will have a considerable bit of lurking affection, in the green places of his heart, for William Browne, and lament that he did not live to become famous. Much of his *Britannia's Pastorals*, as he called them, was written before he was twenty. They were collected into a body of English verse, for the first time, by Anderson; but Davies published an edition in three volumes duodecimo; they have been lately reprinted in two; and the lover of poetry and field-walks, who is not always in a mood for higher stimulants, and who can recognise beauty in a hedge-row elm as well as a forest, may reckon himself lucky in being able to put one of them in his pocket. The pastorals consist of a story with a number of episodes, none of which, or story either, can we ever remember; so we will say nothing more about them. The names of the persons hum in our ears, and we have some conception of two or three of the incidents;

but the scenes in which they take place, the landscapes,
the pastoral images, the idealised country manners,
these are what we are thinking of while the story is
going on ; just as a man should be hearing some local
history while going over meadows and stiles, and
glancing all the while about him instead of paying it
attention.   We shall, therefore, devote this article to
passages marked with our pen ; as the same man might
go over the ground afterwards in other company, and
say, " There is the church I spoke of, in the trees "—
" Yonder is the passage I mentioned, into the wood "
—" Here the ivy full of the singing-birds."   We may,
perhaps, overrate Browne, out of affection for the
things he likes to speak of ; but sometimes his powers
are not to be mistaken.   He calls Cephalus, whom
Aurora loved, him

> *Whose name was worn*
> *Within the bosom of the blushing morn.*

Music is

> *The soul of art, best loved when love is by.*

Raleigh, spoken of under the character of a shepherd,
is a swain

> *Whom all the Graces kissed ;*

and Pan, a god that

> *With gentle nymphs in forests high*
> *Kissed out the sweet time of his infancy.*

That is very beautiful.   Warton, in his *History of*

Poetry, has expressed his admiration of a " charm " in Browne's *Inner Temple Masque*, in which, down by the banks of Lethe, dewdrops are said to be for ever hanging

> On the *limber grass*,
> Poppy and mandragoras ;

and Lethe is described as flowing

> Without coil,
> *Softly, like a stream of oil.*

The fourth eclogue of his *Shepherd's Pipe* is thought, not improbably, to have been in the recollection of Milton, when he wrote *Lycidas*. Like that poem, it is an elegy on the death of a friend. The line marked in the following quatrain might have appeared in *Lycidas*, without any injury to it. It is, indeed, very Miltonic :—

> In deepest passions of my grief-swol'n breast,
> Sweet soul! this only comfort seizeth me,
> That so few years should make thee so much blest,
> *And give such wings to reach eternity.*

In this poem is a description of autumn, in which the different metres are unfortunately but ill-assorted :— they look like bits of elegics begun on different plans ; but the third line of the first quatrain is well felt ; the fourth not unworthy of it ; the watery meadows are capitally painted ; and the closing stanza is like an affecting one taken out of some old English ballad :—

Autumn it was, when droop'd the sweetest flowers,
   And rivers, swollen with pride, o'erlook'd the banks ;
Poor grew the day of summer's golden hours,
   And void of sap stood Ida's cedar ranks.

> The pleasant meadows *sadly lay*
>   *In chill and cooling sweats*
> *By rising fountains,* or as they
>   Fear'd winter's wasteful threats.

> Against the broad-spread oaks
>   Each wind in fury bears ;
> *Yet fell their leaves not half so fast*
>   *As did the shepherd's tears.*

The feeling of analogy between the oak, with its scattered leaves, and the naturally strong man shedding tears for sorrow, is in the best imaginative taste. Had Browne written all thus, he would have found plenty of commentators. The *Shepherd's Pipe* was a somewhat later production than the other pastorals ; and had he lived he would probably have surpassed all that his youth produced. Unfortunately, his mind never appears to have outgrown a certain juvenile ambition of ingenious thoughts and conceits ; and it is these that render it so difficult to make any long quotation from his works. The sixth line in the following is very obscure, perhaps corrupted. But the rest has great liveliness and nature :—

> Look as a lover, with a lingering kiss,
> About to part with the best half that's his ;

Fain would he stay, but that he fears to do it,
And curseth time for so fast hastening to it ;
Now takes his leave, and yet begins anew
To make less vows than are esteem'd true ;
Then says he must be gone, and then doth find
Something he should have spoke that's out of mind ;
And whilst he stands *to look for't in her eyes,*
Their sad sweet glance so ties his faculties
To think from what he parts, that he is now
As far from leaving her, or knowing how,
As when he came ; begins his former strain,
To kiss, to vow, and take his leave again ;
Then turns, comes back, sighs, parts, and yet doth go,
Apt to retire, and loth to leave her so ;—
Brave stream, so part I from thy flowery bank.

Browne is fond of drawing his similes from real, and
even homely life, and often seems to introduce them for
the purpose of giving that kind of variety to a pastoral,
otherwise ideal ; for though the title of his poem is
British, and the scene also, it is in other respects
Arcadian and Pagan. The effect is somewhat jarring ;
and yet it is impossible to quarrel with the particular
descriptions :—

As children on a play-day leave the schools,
And gladly run into the swimming pools ;
Or in the thickets, all with nettles stung,
Rush to despoil some sweet thrush of her young ;
Or with their hats for fish lade in a brook
Withouten pain ; but when the morn doth look
Out of the eastern gates, a snail would faster
Glide to the schools, than they unto their master ;
So when before I sung the songs of birds, &c.

The following is a complete picture :—

> —As a nimble squirrel from the wood,
> Ranging the hedges for his filbert food,
> Sits partly on a bough, his brown nuts cracking,
> And from the shell the sweet white kernel taking,
> Till, with their crooks and bags, a sort of boys
> To share with him, come with so great a noise,
> That he is forced to leave a nut nigh broke,
> And for his life leap to a neighbour oak,
> Thence to a beech, thence to a row of ashes,
> Whilst through the quagmires and red water plashes
> The boys run dabbling through thick and thin ;
> One tears his hose, another breaks his shin ;
> This, torn and tattered, hath with much ado
> Got to the briers, and that hath lost his shoe ;
> This dropt his band, that headlong falls for haste,
> *Another cries behind for being last ;*
> With sticks and stones, and many a sounding hollow,
> The little pool with no small sport they follow,
> Whilst he from tree to tree, from spray to spray
> Gets to the wood, and hides him in his dray ;
> Such shift made Riot, ere he could get up, &c.

Here is another picture, still homelier, but equally complete, and as robust in its full-grown strength as the other is light and boyish :—

> As when a smith and's man (lame Vulcan's fellows),
> Called from the anvil or the puffing bellows
> To clap a well-wrought shoe, for more than pay,
> Upon a stubborn nag of Galloway,
> Or unback'd jennet, or a Flanders mare,
> That at the forge stands snuffing of the air ;
> *The swarthy smith spits in his buck-horn fist,*

And bids his men bring out the five-fold twist,
His shackles, shacklocks, hampers, gyves, and chains,
His linkèd bolts; and with no little pains
These make him fast; and lest all these should faulter,
Unto a post, with some six-doubled halter,
He binds his head; yet all are of the least
To curb the fury of the headstrong beast;
When, if a carrier's jade be brought unto him,
His man can hold his foot while he can shoe him;
Remorse was so enforced to bind him stronger.

This is a Dutch picture, or one that Mr. Crabbe
might have admired. The following might have
adorned the pages of Spenser himself. The ascension
of the fogs and mists, and the cessation of all noise, are
in a true—nay, in a high spirit of grandeur; and the
very delicacy of the conclusion adds to it. The sense
of hushing solemnity is drawn to the finest point:—

Now great Hyperion left his golden throne,
That on the dancing waves in glory shone;
For whose declining on the western shore
The oriental hills black mantles wore;
And thence apace the gentle twilight fled,
That had from hideous caverns usherèd
All-drowsy Night; who in a car of jet,
By steeds of iron-grey (which mainly sweat
Moist drops on all the world) drawn through the sky.
The helps of darkness waited orderly.
First, thick clouds rose from all the liquid plains;
Then mists from marishes, and grounds whose veins
Were conduit-pipes to many a crystal spring;
From standing pools and fens were following

Unhealthy fogs ; each river, every rill,
Sent up their vapours to attend her will.
These pitchy curtains drew 'twixt earth and heaven,
And as Night's chariot through the air was driven,
Clamour grew dumb ; unheard was shepherd's song,
And silence girt the woods : no warbling tongue
Talk'd to the echo ; satyrs broke their dance,
And all the upper world lay in a trance ;
Only the curling streams soft chidings kept :
And little gales, that from the green leaf swept
Dry summer's dust, in fearful whisp'ring stirr'd
As loth to waken any singing bird.

Browne was a Devonshire man, and is supposed to
have died at Ottery St. Mary, the birthplace of Coleridge.
He was not unworthy to have been the countryman of
that exquisite observer of Nature, himself a pastoral man,
though he wrote no pastorals ; for Coleridge not only
preferred a country to a town life, but his mind as well
as his body (when it was not with Plato and the school-
men) delighted to live in woody places, " enfolding," as
he beautifully says,

Sunny spots of greenery.

And how many other great and good men have there
not been, with whom the humblest lover of Arcady may,
in this respect, claim fellowship ?—men, nevertheless,
fond of town also, and of the most active and busy life,
when it was their duty to enter it. The most universal
genius must of necessity include the green districts of

the world in his circle, otherwise he would not run it a third part round. Shakspeare himself, prosperous manager as he was, retired to his native place before he was old. Do we think that, with all his sociality, his chief companions there were such as a country town afforded ? Depend upon it, they were the trees, and the fields, and his daughter Susanna. Be assured, that no gentleman of the place was seen so often pacing the banks of the Avon, sitting on the stiles in the meadows, looking with the thrush at the sunset, or finding

Books in the running brooks,
Sermons in stones, and good in everything.

Cervantes, the Shakspeare of Spain, (for if his poetry answered but to one small portion of Shakspeare, his prose made up the rest,) proclaims his truly pastoral heart, notwithstanding his satire, not only in his *Galatea*, but in a hundred passages of *Don Quixote*, particularly the episodes. He delighted equally in knowledge of the world and the most ideal poetic life. It is easy to see, by the stories of *Marcella* and *Leandra*, that this great writer wanted little to have become a Quixote himself, in the Arcadian line! Nothing but the extremest good sense supplied him a proper balance in this respect for his extreme romance.

Boccaccio was another of these great child-like minds, whose knowledge of the world is ignorantly confounded

with a devotion to it.   See, in his *Admetus*, and
Theseid, and *Genealogia Deorum*, &c., and in the
Decameron itself, how he revels in groves and gardens;
and how, when he begins making a list of trees, he
cannot leave off.   Doubtless, he had been of a more
sensual temperament than Cervantes; but his faith
remained unshaken in the highest things.   His veins
might have contained an excess of the genial; but so did
his heart.   When the priest threatened him in advanced
life with the displeasure of Heaven, he was shocked and
alarmed, and obliged to go to Petrarch for comfort.

Chaucer was a courtier, and a companion of princes;
nay, a reformer also, and a stirrer out in the world.   He
understood that world, too, thoroughly, in the ordinary
sense of such understanding; yet, as he was a true great
poet in everything, so in nothing more was he so than
in loving the country, and the trees and fields.   It is as
hard to get him out of a grove as his friend Boccaccio;
and he tells us, that, in May, he would often go out into
the meadows to " abide " there, solely in order to " look
upon the daisy."   Milton seems to have made a point
of never living in a house that had not a garden to it.

A certain amount of trusting goodness, surviving
twice the worldly knowledge possessed by those who
take scorn for superiority, is the general characteristic
of men of this stamp, whether of the highest order of

that stamp or not. Cowley, Thomson, and Shenstone were such men. Shenstone was deficient in animal spirits, and condescended to be vexed when people did not come to see his retirement ; but few men had an acuter discernment of the weak points of others and the general mistakes of mankind, as anybody may see by his *Essays* ; and yet in those *Essays* he tells us, that he never passed a town or village, without regretting that he could not make the acquaintance of some of the good people that lived there. Thomson's whole poetry may be said to be pastoral, and everybody knows what a good fellow he was ; how beloved by his friends ; how social, and yet how sequestered ; and how he preferred a house but a floor high at Richmond (for that which is now shown as his, was then a ground-floor only), to one of more imposing dimensions amidst

> The smoke and stir of this dim spot,
> Which men call *London*.

Cowley was a partisan, a courtier, a diplomatist ; nay, a satirist, and an admirable one, too. See his *Cutter of Coleman Street*, the gaiety and sharpness of which no one suspects who thinks of him only in the ordinary peacefulness of his reputation ; though, doubtless, he would have been the first man to do a practical kindness to any of the Puritans whom he laughed at. His friends the Cavaliers thought he laughed at themselves, in this

very comedy; so much more did he gird hypocrisy and
pretension in general than in the particular : but Charles
the Second said of him after his death, that he had
" not left a better man behind him in England." His
partisanship, his politics, his clever satire, his once
admired " metaphysical " poetry, as Johnson calls it,
nobody any longer cares about ; but still, as Pope said,

> We love the language of his heart.

He has become a sort of poetical representative of all
the love that existed of groves and gardens in those days
—of parterres, and orchards, and stately old houses ;
but above all, of the cottage ; a taste for which, as a
gentleman's residence, seems to have originated with
him, or at least been first avowed by him ; for we can
trace it no farther back. " A small house and a large
garden" was his aspiration; and he obtained it. Somebody, unfortunately, has got our Cowley's *Essays*—we
don't reproach him, for it is a book to keep a good while ;
but they contain a delightful passage on this subject,
which should have been quoted. Take, however, an extract or two from the verses belonging to those *Essays.*
They will conclude this part of our subject well :

> Hail, old patrician trees, so great and good !
> Hail, ye plebeian underwood !
> Where the poetic birds rejoice,
> And for their quiet nests and plenteous food,
> Pay with their grateful voice.

Here let me, careless and unthoughtful lying,
  Hear the soft winds above me flying,
  With all their wanton boughs dispute,
And the more tuneful birds to both replying,
  Nor be myself, too, mute.

Ah ! wretched and too solitary he,
  Who loves not his own company !
  He'll feel the weight of it many a day,
Unless he call in sin or vanity,
  To help to bear 't away.

  * * * *   *

When Epicurus to the world had taught
  That Pleasure was the Chiefest Good,
(And was, perhaps, i' th' right, if rightly understood,)
  His life he to his doctrine brought,
And in a garden's shade that sovereign pleasure sought.

  * * * * * *

Where does the wisdom and the power divine
In a more bright and sweet reflection shine—
Where do we finer strokes and colours see
Of the Creator's real poetry,
Than when we with attention look
Upon the third day's volume of the book?
If we could open and *intend* our eye,
We all, like Moses, should espy,
Ev'n in a bush, the radiant Deity.

  * * * * *

Methinks I see great Diocletian walk
  In the Salonian garden's noble shade,
  Which by his own imperial hands was made.
I see him smile, methinks, as he does talk
  With the ambassadors, who come in vain
  To entice him to a throne again.

" If I, my friends," said he, " should to you show
All the delights which in these gardens grow,
'Tis likelier much that you should with me stay,
Than 'tis that you should carry me away ;
And trust me not, my friends, if every day
I walk not here with more delight,
Than ever, after the most happy fight,
In triumph to the capitol I rode,
To thank the gods, and to be thought, myself, almost a god."

A noble line that—long and stately as the triumph which it speaks of. Yet the Emperor and the Poet agreed in preferring a walk down an alley of roses. There was nothing so much calculated to rebuke or bewilder them there, as in the faces of their fellow-creatures, even after the " happiest fight."

1402

CHAPTER X.
RETURN TO SICILY AND MOUNT ÆTNA.

SUBJECT OF MOUNT ÆTNA RESUMED :—ITS BEAUTIES—ITS
HORRORS—REASON WHY PEOPLE ENDURE THEM.—LOVE-
STORY OF AN EARTHQUAKE.

IN now emphatically returning to Sicily, though we have never been entirely absent from it, while discussing the pastoral poets of other countries, we

12

shall round our subject properly by finishing the circle where we began it; and in order to render our plan as complete as possible, we have not been without a sense of chronological order. In resuming, therefore, the subject of Ætna, we proceed to regard the mountain in relation to the impression it makes on modern times and existing inhabitants.

The reader is aware that our Jar was not intended to be associated with nothing but sweets. Bees, it was observed, extract honey from the bitterest as well as sweetest flowers; and we only stipulated, as they do, for a sweet result;—for something, which by the fact of its being deducible from bitterness, shows the tendency of Nature to that dulcet end, and gives a lesson to her creature man to take thought and warning, and do as much for himself. In truth, were man heartily to do so, and leave off asking Nature to superintend everything for him, and take the trouble off his hands, which it seems a manifest condition of things that she should not (man looking very like an experiment to see how far he can develop the energies of which he is composed, and prove himself worthy of continuance), how are we to know that he would not get rid of all such evils as do not appear to be necessary to his well-being, and, in the language of the great Eastern poet, make " the morning stars sing for joy?"—sing for joy, that another heaven

is added to their list. Mount Ætna, for instance, which
is one of the safety-valves of the globe, does not *force*
people to live within the sphere of its operations. Why,
therefore, should they? Why do not the inhabitants of
Catania and other places migrate, as nations have done
from the face of an enemy or famine, and plant themselves elsewhere? When the convulsion comes, and
destruction hovers over them, the saints are implored as
the gods were of old, and everything is referred to the
ordinances of Heaven. But the saints might answer,
" Why do you continue to live here, in the teeth of
these repeated warnings? Why cannot the earth have
safety-valves, but you must needs plant yourselves right
in the way of them, as infants may do with steam-
engines?" This is the honey that might be extracted
from the bitter past. On the other hand, if this be idle
speculation, and the reason of the thing be on the side
of continuing to implore the saints and perishing in
earthquakes, then Nature, who is always determined to
have no evil unmixed, suggests topics of consolation
from the greater amount of good ; from the far longer
duration of the periods of serenity and joy around the
mountain, compared with those of convulsion ; and from
all those images of beauty and abundance, which produce another honey against the bitterness of what
cannot be altered. The bee himself, like the nightin-

gale and the dove, and other beautiful creatures, is an inhabitant of Ætna. The fires of the mountain help to produce some of his sweetest thyme. The energetic little, warmth-loving, honey-making, armed, threatening, murmuring, bitter-sweet, and useful creature, seems like one of the particles of the mountain, gifted with wings. We might as well have brought our honey from Mount Ætna as Mount Hybla, and very likely it actually came thence; only the latter, like Mount Hymettus, is identified with the word, and its supposed district still famous for the product. In fact (though the name seems to be no longer retained anywhere) there were several Hyblas of old, one of them at the foot of Ætna; so that our Jar may come from both places. The word, which is older than Greek, was probably Phœnician, from a root signifying mellifluence; unless it originated in the sound of the bubbling of brooks, of the neighbourhood of which bees are fond.

We cannot quit Mount Ætna without saying something more of it, especially as it has lately been in action, not without hints of its operation as far as Scotland, where there have been many shocks of earthquake. Everybody knows that Ætna is the greatest volcano in Europe, some twenty miles in ascent from Catania, and with a circumference for its base of between eighty and ninety. All the climates of the world are

there, except those of the African desert. At the foot
are the palms and aloes of the tropics, with the corn,
wine, and oil of Italy. The latter continue for fourteen
or fifteen miles of ascent. Then come the chestnuts of
Spain, then the beeches of England, then the firs of
Norway—the whole forest-belt being five or six miles
in ascent, interspersed with park-like scenery, and the
most magnificent pastures. Singing-birds, and flocks
and herds are there, with abundance of game. The
remainder, a thousand feet high, is a naked peak,
covered for the greater part of the year with snow, but
often hot to the feet in the midst of it, toilsome to
ascend, and terminating in the great crater, miles
in circumference, fuming and blind with smoke—the
largest of several others. The whole mountain, with
an enormous chasm in its side four or five miles broad,
stands in the midst of six-and-thirty subject mountains,
"each a Vesuvius," generated by its awful parent.
Horror and loveliness prevail throughout it, alternately,
or together. You look from mountain to mountain,
over tremendous depths, to the most beautiful woody
scenery. The lowest region is a paradise, betraying
black grounds of lava, and beds of ashes, which remind
you to what it is liable. The top is a ghastly white
peak, shivering with cold, though it is a mouth for fire,
but lovely at a distance in the light of the moon at

night, and presenting a view from it by day, especially
at sunrise, which baffles description with ecstasy. Count,
Stolberg, a German poet, who beheld this spectacle in
the year 1792, when the mountain was in action, says,
that by the dawning light of the day he saw nothing
round about him but snow and black ashes, vast masses
of lava, and a smoking crater, together with a huge
bed of clouds, the darkening extremities of which the
eye could not clearly distinguish either from the mountains or the sea, " *till the majestic sun rose in fire, and
reduced every object to order.*—Chaos seemed to unfold
itself, where no four-footed beast, no bird, interrupted
the solemn silence of the formless void :

Wo sie keinen Todten begruben, und keiner erstehen wird,

as Klopstock says of the ice-encircled pole :

No dead are buried there ; nor any there will rise.

"Ætna cast his black shades," continues he, "over
the grey dawn of the western atmosphere; while round
him stood his sons, but far beneath, yet volcanic mountains all, in number six-and-thirty, each a Vesuvius.
To the north, the east, and the south, Sicily lay at our
feet, with its hills, and rivers, and lakes, and cities. In
the low deep, the clouds, tinged with purple, were dis-
persed and vanished from the presence of the golden

sun ; while their shades flying before the west wind, were scattered over the landscape far and wide." *

Mr. Hughes's description is minuter, yet still more effective. "At length," says he, "faint streaks of light, shooting athwart the horizon, which became brighter and brighter, announced the approach of the great luminary ; and when he sprang up in his majesty, supported on a throne of radiant clouds, that fine scriptural image of the giant rejoicing to run his course, flashed across my mind. As he ascended in the sky, the mountain tops began to stream with golden light, and new beauties successively developed themselves, until day dawned upon the Catanian plains. Sicily then lay expanded like a map beneath our eyes, presenting a very curious effect ; nearly all its mountains could be descried, with the many cities that surmount their summits ; more than half its coasts, with their bays, indentations, towns, and promontories, could be traced, as well as the entire course of rivers, sparkling like silver bands that encircle the valleys and the plains. Add to this the rich tints of so delightful an atmosphere ; add the dark blue tract of sea rolling its mysterious waves, as it were, into infinite space ; add that spirit of antiquity which lingers in these charming scenes, in-

---

* *Travels through Germany, Switzerland, Italy*, &c. Translated by Holcroft, vol. iv. p. 298.

fusing a soul into the features of nature, as expression lights up a beautiful countenance; and where will you find a scene to rival that which is viewed from Ætna?"*

Compare this spectacle with one of the great eruptions, and the agonising days that precede it. Smoke and earthquake commence them. The days are darkened; the nights are sleepless and horrible, and seem ten times as long as usual. People rush to the churches in prayer, or crowd the doorways (which are thought the safest places), or remain out of doors in boats or carriages. Religious processions move in terror through the streets. Sometimes the air is blackened with a powder, sometimes with ashes, which fall and gather everywhere, such as Pompeii was buried with. Lightnings play about Ætna; the sea rises against the dark atmosphere, in ghastly white billows; dreadful noises succeed, accompanied with thunder, like batteries of artillery; the earth rocks; landslips take place down the hill-sides, carrying whole fields and homesteads into other men's grounds; cities are overthrown, burying shrieking thousands. At length, the mountain bursts out in flame and lava, perhaps in forty or fifty places at once, the principal crater throwing out hot glowing stones, which have been known to be carried eighteen

---

* Quoted in Evans's *Classic and Connoisseur in Italy and Sicily*, vol. ii. p. 358.

miles, and the frightful mineral torrent running forth
in streams of fiery red, pouring down into the plains,
climbing over walls, effacing estates, and rushing into
and usurping part of the bed of the sea. A river of
lava has been known to be fifty feet deep, and four miles
broad.* Fancy such a stream coming towards London,
as wide as from Marylebone to Mile End! By degrees,
the lava thickens into a black and rustling semi-liquid,
rather pushed along than flowing; though its heat
has been found lingering after a lapse of eight years.
When the survivors of all these horrors gather breath,
and look back upon time and place, they find houses
and families abolished, and have to begin, as it were,
their stunned existence anew.

Yet they build again over these earthquakes. They
inhabit and delight in this mountain. Catania, the
city at its foot, which has been several times de-
molished, is one of the gayest in Italy.

How is this?

The reason is, that all pain, generally speaking, is
destined to be short and fugitive, compared with the
duration of a greater amount of pleasure;—that the
souls which perish in the convulsion, were partakers of
that pleasure for the greater part of their lives, perhaps
the gayest of the gay city;—that all of them were born

* Swinburne's *Travels in the Two Sicilies*, vol. iv. p. 148.

there, or connected with it;—that it is inconvenient, perhaps without government aid impossible, to remove, and commence business elsewhere;—that they do not think the catastrophe likely to recur soon, perhaps not in the course of their lives;—nay, that possibly there may be something of a gambling excitement,—of the stimulus of a mixture of hope and fear,—in thus living on the borders of life and death—of this great snap-dragon bowl of Europe—especially surrounded as they are with the old familiar scenes, and breathing a joyous atmosphere.   But undoubtedly the chief reasons are necessity, real or supposed, and the natural tendency of mankind to make the best of their position and turn their thoughts from sadness.   So the Catanian goes to his dinner, and builds a new ball-room *out of the lava!*

Perhaps the most touching of all the consolations to be met with in the history of these catastrophes, is the testimony they bear to the maternal affections.   The men who perish from the overthrow of houses are said to be generally found in attitudes of resistance:—the women are bent double over their children.   The great vindication of evil is, that (constituted as we are) we could not know so much joy, nor manifest so much virtue without it; and certainly, in instances like these, it fetches out, under circumstances of the extremest weakness, the most beautiful strength of the human heart. Still, such wholesale trials of it do not appear to be demanded by any unavoidable necessity. The fact forces itself upon the mind, that human beings need not continue to live in such places, and that the geological well-being of the globe does not demand it. As to animals of the inferior creation, who are destroyed at these times, assuredly they know almost as little about it till the last moment, as the lamb who licks the hand of his slayer; and as soon as the mountain is cleared, the larks and nightingales are again singing, and the bees enjoying the flowers in its most awful ravines.

For months, for years, sometimes for a hundred years and more, perhaps for many hundreds, this tremendous phenomenon is quiet. Homer does not seem to have heard of its burning. The volcano first makes its appearance in Pindar. Theocritus knew its capabilities well; yet he speaks of it as nothing but a seat of pastoral felicity. His Polyphemus contrasts its serenity with the dangers of the sea; and another of his shepherds, in answer to an observation about fathers and mothers, says to a shepherd of the plains, that Ætna is *his* mother, and that he is as rich in sheep and goats as the latter fancies himself to be during dreams. The first recorded eruption of Ætna was in the time of Empedocles, about five hundred years before Christ; and from that time to the year 1819 inclusive, a French writer has calculated that there have been seventy-two others *mentioned*.* We cannot say how many more have ensued. The one that not long ago took place was harmless, we believe, as far as lives were concerned, except to some rash persons who were too anxious to see the effect of the lava upon a pool of water. The pool turned into steam, and scalded them. Slight eruptions are little regarded, and indeed are little dangerous compared with what precedes them. The worst peril is the earthquake. The lava, though an ugly customer, can be safelier treated with. Even slight earthquakes are not much heeded, after the first alarm. Mr. Vaughan, an English traveller in the year 1810, says, that upon his going into the town of Messina, after a slight shock, from his country-lodging, and approaching the carriages in which some ladies were sitting in expectation of another, he said to one of them, an acquaintance of his, "Is it not shocking?" "It is indeed very shocking," said the lady. "*You were not at the Opera!*" † Humboldt speaks of a young lady in South America, who was so accustomed to these visitations, that she thought the topic vulgar. She expressed a wish that people would leave off talking about "these nasty earthquakes."

---

* *Voyage Critique à l'Ætna*, tom. i. p. 529.

† Vide the Letters appended to a *View of the Present State of Italy*, translated from the Italian, by Thomas Wright Vaughan, Esq., p. 70.

If you tell a Sicilian that there are no earthquakes in England, he acknowledges, of course, the merit of their absence, but smiles to think that you can suppose it a compensation for the want of vines and olives. The following amusing conversation took place in an inn, between the English traveller just mentioned and a priest and his landlady, at Caltagirone. The priest, "after many apologies for the liberty he was taking," says Mr. Vaughan, "begged to converse with me upon the subject of England, which the people of these parts were very anxious to hear about, as the opportunity of inquiring so seldom occurred; and, by the time I had dined, I observed a dozen people collected round the door, with their eyes and mouths open, to hear the examination.

" 'And pray, Signor, is it true what we are told, that you have no olives in England ? ' *

" ' Yes, perfectly true.'

" ' Cospetto! how so ? '

" ' Cospettone !' † said the lady.

" 'Our climate is not propitious to the growth of the olive.'

" ' But then, Signor, for oranges ! '

* " Olives and bread form the principal part of the food of the lower classes in Sicily, and oil is a necessary of life."

† " About equivalent to ' zounds ' and ' gadzooks.' "

" ' We have no oranges neither.'

" ' *Poveretto!* ' said the landlady, with a tone of compassion ; which is a sort of fondling diminutive of ' *Povero*,' ' Poor creature,' or as you would say to your child, ' Poor little fellow ! '

" 'But how is that possible, Signor?' said the priest. ' Have you no fruit in your country ? '

" ' We have very fine fruit ; but our winters are severe, and not genial enough for the orange-tree.'

" ' That is just what they told me,' said the lady, ' at Palermo, that England is all snow, and a great many stones.'

" ' But then, Signor, we have heard, what we can scarcely believe, that you have not any wine ? '

" ' It is perfectly true. We have vines that bear fruit ; but the sun in our climate is not sufficiently strong, which must be boiling, as it is here, to produce any wine.'

" ' Then, Jesu Maria ! how the deuce do you do ? '

" I told them that, notwithstanding, we got on pretty well ; that we had some decent sort of mutton, and very tolerable-looking beef ; that our poultry was thought eatable, and our bread pretty good ; that, instead of wine, we had a thing they call ale, which our people, here and there, seemed to relish exceedingly ; and that, by the help of these articles, a good *constitu-*

tion, and the blessing of God, our men were as hardy, and as loyal and brave, and our women as accomplished, and virtuous, and handsome, as any other people, I believed, under heaven.

"'Besides, Mr. Abbate, I beg leave to ask you, what cloth is your coat of?'

"'*Cospetto!* it is English!' with an air of importance.

"'And your hat?'

"'Why, that's English.'

"'And this lady's gown, and her bonnet and ribbons?'

"'Why, they are English.'

"'All English. Then you see how it is: we send you, in exchange for what we don't grow, half the comforts and conveniences you enjoy in your island. Besides, *padrona mia gentile* (my agreeable landlady), we can never regret that we don't grow these articles, since it ensures us an intercourse with a nation we esteem!'

"'*Viva!*' ('Long life to you'), said the landlady, and '*Bravo!*' said the priest; and between *bravo* and *viva*, the best friends in the world, I escaped to my lettiga (litter)." *

We must close this article with a love-story, in connexion with the dreadful earthquake of 1783, which

* *View of Italy*, ut supra, p. 79.

destroyed Messina, and swept into the sea, *in one moment*, nearly three thousand persons on the opposite coast of Scylla, together with their prince.* The reader may believe as much of the love as he pleases, but the extraordinary circumstance on which it turns is only one of a multitude of phenomena, all true and marvellous.

Giuseppe, a young vine-grower in a village at the foot of the mountains looking towards Messina, was in love with Maria, the daughter of the richest bee-master of the place; and his affection, to the great displeasure of the father, was returned. The old man, though he had encouraged him at first, wished her to marry a young profligate in the city, because the latter was richer and of a higher stock; but the girl had a great deal of good sense as well as feeling; and the father was puzzled how to separate them, the families having been long acquainted. He did everything in his power to render the visits of the lover uncomfortable to both parties; but as they saw through his object, and love can endure a great deal, he at length thought himself compelled to make use of insult. Contriving, therefore, one day to proceed from one mortifying word to

---

* It is calculated that 40,000 souls perished in this convulsion. In the greatest of all the Sicilian earthquakes, that of 1693, the earth shook but four minutes, and overthrew almost all the towns on the eastern side of the island.

another, he took upon him, as if in right of offence, to anticipate his daughter's attention to the parting guest, and show him out of the door himself, adding a broad hint that it might be as well if he did not return very soon.

" Perhaps, Signor Antonio," said the youth, piqued at last to say something harsh himself, " you do not wish the son of your old friend to return at all ? "

" Perhaps not," said the bee-master.

" What," said the poor lad, losing all the courage of his anger in the terrible thought of his never having any more of those beautiful lettings out of the door by Maria,—"what! do you mean to say I may not hope to be invited again, even by yourself?—that you yourself will never again invite me, or come to see me ? "

" Oh, we shall all come, of course, to the great Signor Giuseppe," said the old man, looking scornful,— " all cap in hand."

" Nay, nay," returned Giuseppe, in a tone of pro-pitiation ; " I'll wait till you do me the favour to look in some morning, in the old way, and have a chat about the French ; and perhaps," added he, blushing, "you will then bring Maria with you, as you used to do ; and I won't attempt to see her till then."

" Oh, we'll all come of course," said Antonio, im-patiently; "cat, dog, and all; and when we *do*," added

he, in a very significant tone, "you may come again
yourself."

Giuseppe tried to laugh at this jest, and thus still
propitiate him; but the old man hastening to shut the
door, angrily cried, "Ay, cat, dog, and all, and the
cottage besides, with Maria's dowry along with it; and
then you may come again, *and not till then.*"   And so
saying, he banged the door, and giving a furious look
at poor Maria, went into another room to scrawl a
note to the young citizen.

The young citizen came in vain, and Antonio grew
sulkier and angrier every day, till at last he turned his
bitter jest into a vow; exclaiming with an oath, that
Giuseppe should never have his daughter, till he (the
father), daughter, dog, cat, cottage, bee-hives, and all,
with her dowry of almond-trees to boot, set out some
fine morning to beg the young vine-dresser to accept
them.

Poor Maria grew thin and pale, and Giuseppe looked
little better, turning all his wonted jests into sighs, and
often interrupting his work to sit and look towards the
said almond-trees, which formed a beautiful clump on
an ascent upon the other side of the glen, sheltering the
best of Antonio's bee-hives, and composing a pretty
dowry for the pretty Maria, which the father longed to
see in possession of the flashy young citizen.

One morning, after a very sultry night, as the poor youth sat endeavouring to catch a glimpse of her in this direction, he observed that the clouds gathered in a very unusual manner over the country, and then hung low in the air, heavy and immovable. Towards Messina the sky looked so red, that at first he thought the city on fire, till an unusual heat affecting him, and a smell of sulphur arising, and the little river at his feet assuming a tinge of a muddy ash-colour, he knew that some convulsion of the earth was at hand. His first impulse was a wish to cross the ford, and, with mixed anguish and delight, to find himself again in the cottage of Antonio, giving the father and daughter all the help in his power. A tremendous burst of thunder and lightning startled him for a moment; but he was proceeding to cross, when his ears tingled, his head turned giddy, and while the earth heaved beneath his feet, he saw the opposite side of the glen lifted up with a horrible deafening noise, and then the cottage itself, with all around it, cast, as he thought, to the ground, and buried for ever. The sturdy youth, for the first time in his life, fainted away. When his senses returned, he found himself pitched back into his own premises, but not injured, the blow having been broken by the vines.

But on looking in horror towards the site of the cottage up the hill, what did he see there? or rather,

what did he *not* see there ?   And what *did* he see,
forming a new mound, furlongs down the side of the
hill, almost at the bottom of the glen, and in his own
homestead ?

Antonio's cottage :—Antonio's cottage, with the
almond-trees, and the bee-hives, and the very cat and
dog, and the old man himself, and the daughter (both
senseless), all come, as if, in the father's words, to beg
him to accept them !   Such awful pleasantries, so to
speak, sometimes take place in the middle of Nature's
deepest tragedies, and such exquisite good may spring
out of evil.

For it was so in the end, if not in the intention.
The old man (who, together with his daughter, had only
been stunned by terror) was superstitiously frightened
by the dreadful circumstance, if not affectionately moved
by the attentions of the son of his old friend, and the
delight and religious transport of his child.   Besides,
though the cottage and the almond-trees, and the
bee-hives, had all come miraculously safe down the
hill (a phenomenon which has frequently occurred
in these extraordinary *landslips*), the flower-gardens,
on which his bees fed, were almost all destroyed ;
his property was lessened, his pride lowered ; and
when the convulsion was well over, and the guitars
were again playing in the valley, he consented to

become the inmate, for life, of the cottage of the enchanted couple.

He could never attain, however, to the innate delicacy of his child, and he would sometimes, with a petu-
lant sigh, intimate at table what a pity it was that she
had not married the rich and high-feeding citizen. At
such times as these, Maria would gather one of her
husband's feet between her own under the table, and
with a squeeze of it that repaid him tenfold for the
mortification, would steal a look at him which said, " I
possess all which it is possible for me to desire."

CHAPTER XI.

BEES.

IT would be ungrateful and impossible, in the course of so sweet and generous a theme as our Jar of Honey has furnished us with, not to devote a portion of it to the cause of all its sweetness—the Bee. We are not going, however, to repeat more common-place in its eulogy than we can help. The grounds of the admiration of nature are without end; and as to those matters of fact or

science which appear to be settled—nay, even most
settled—some new theory is coming up every day, in
these extraordinary times, to compel us to think the
points over again, and doubt whether we are quite so
knowing as we supposed. Not only are bee-masters
disputing the discoveries of Huber respecting the operations of the hive, but searchers into nature seem almost
prepared to re-open the old question respecting the
equivocal generation of the bee, and set the electrical
experiments of Mr. Cross at issue with the conclusions
of Redi.

How this may turn out, we know not; but sure we
are, that it will be a long time indeed before the praise
and glory of the bee can have exhausted its vocabulary
—before people cry out to authors, " Say no more; you
have said too much already of its wonderfulness—too
much of the sweetness and beauty of its productions."
Too much, we are of opinion, cannot be said of any
marvel in nature, unless it be trivial or false. The old
prosaical charge against hyperbolical praises of the
beautiful, we hold to be naught. Ask a lover, and he
will say, and say truly, that no human terms can do
justice to the sweetness in his mistress's eyes—to the
virgin bloom on her cheek. If words could equal them,
Nature would hardly be our superior. Hear what is
said on the point by Marlowe :—

If all the pens that ever poets held
Had fed the feelings of their masters' thoughts,
And every sweetness that inspired their hearts,
Their minds, and muses on admired themes;
If all the heavenly quintessence they 'stil
From their immortal flowers of poesy,
Wherein, as in a mirror, we perceive
The highest reaches of a human wit:
If these had made one poem's period,
And all combined in beauty's worthiness,
Yet should there hover in their restless heads
One thought, one grace, one wonder, at the least,
Which into words no virtue can digest.

Did any one ever sufficiently admire the *entire elegance* of the habits and pursuits of bees? their extraction of nothing but the quintessence of the flowers; their preference of those that have the finest and least adulterated odour; their avoidance of everything squalid (so unlike flies); their eager ejection or exclusion of it from the hive, as in the instance of carcases of intruders, which, if they cannot drag away, they cover up and entomb; their love of clean, quiet, and delicate neighbourhoods, thymy places with brooks; their singularly clean management of so liquid and adhesive a thing as honey, from which they issue forth to their work as if they had had nothing to do with it; their combination with honey-making of the elegant manufacture of wax, of which they make their apartments, and which is used

by mankind for none but patrician or other choice pur-
poses; their orderly policy; their delight in sunshine;
their attention to one another; their apparent indifference to everything purely regarding themselves, apart
from the common good? A writer of elegant Italian
verse, who recast the book of Virgil on Bees, has taken
occasion of their supposed dislike of places abounding
in *echoes,* to begin his poem with a pretty conceit. He
was one of the first of his countrymen who ventured
to dispense with rhyme; and he makes the bees themselves send him a deputation, on purpose to admonish
him not to use it:—

> Mentre era per cantare i vostri doni
> Con alte rime, o verginette caste,
> Vaghe angelette de le erbose rive,
> Preso dal sonno in sul spuntar de l' alba,
> M' apparve un coro de la vostra gente,
> E da la lingua onde s' accoglie il mele,
> Sciolsono in chiara voce este parole:—
> " O spirto amico, che dopo mill' anni
> E cinquecento rinnovar ti piace
> E le nostre fatiche e i nostri studi,
> Fuggi le rime e 'l rimbombar sonoro.

> " Tu sai pur che l' immagin de la voce,
> Che risponde dai sassi ov' Eco alberga,
> Sempre nimica fù del nostro regno:
> Non sai tu ch' ella fù conversa in pietra,
> E fù inventrice de le prime rime?
> E dei saper, ch' ove abita costei,

Null' ape abitar può per l' importuno
Ed imperfetto suo parlar loquace."

Cosi diss' egli : poi tra labbro e labbro
Mi pose un favo di soave mele,
E lieto se n' andò volando al cielo.
Ond' io, da tal divinità spirato,
Non temerò cantare i vostri onori
Con verso Etrusco da le rime sciolto.

E canterò, come il soave mele,
Celeste don, sopra i fioretti e l' erba
L' aere distilla liquido e sereno ;
E come l' api industriose e caste
L' adunino, e con studio e con ingegno
Dappoi compongan le odorate cere,
Per onorar l' immagine di Dio ;—
Spettacoli ed effetti vaghi e rari,
Di maraviglie pieni e di bellezze.

— *Le Api* del RUCELLAI.

While bent on singing your delightful gifts
In lofty rhyme, O little virgins chaste,
Sweet little angels of the flowery brooks,
Sleep seized me on the golden point of morn,
And I beheld a choir of your small people,
Who, with the tongue with which they take the honey,
Buzz'd forth in the clear air these earnest words :—
"O friendly soul, that after the long lapse
Of thrice five hundred years, dost please thee sing
Our toils and art, shun—shun, we pray thee, rhyme :
Shun rhyme, and its rebounding noise.   Full well
Thou know'st, that the invisible voice which sits
Answering to calls in rocks, Echo by name,
Was hostile to us ever ; and thou know'st—

Or dost thou not ?—that she, who was herself
Turn'd to a hollow rock, first found out rhyme.
Learn further then, that wheresoe'er she dwells,
No bee can dwell, for very hate and dread
Of her importunate and idle babble."

Such were the words that issued from that choir ;
Then 'twixt my lips they put some honey drops,
And so in gladness took their flight aloft.
Whence I, with such divinity made strong,
Doubt not, O bees, to sing your race renown'd
In Tuscan verse, freed from the clangs of rhyme.
Yea, I will sing how the celestial boon,
Honey, by some sweet mystery of the dew,
Is born of air in bosoms of the flowers,
Liquid, serene ; and how the diligent bees
Collect it, working further with such art,
That odorous tapers thence deck holy shrines.
O sights, and O effects, lovely and strange !
Full of the marvellous and the beautiful !

—*The Bees* of RUCELLAI.

The reader need not be told, that the tapers here alluded to are those which adorn Catholic altars. Rucellai was a kinsman of Pope Leo the Tenth and his successor Clement ; and his first mode of bespeaking favour for his bees was by associating them with the offices of the church. Beautiful are those tapers, without doubt ; and well might the poet express his admiration at their being the result of the work of the little unconscious insect, who compounded the material. So,

in every wealthy house in England, every evening,
where lamps do not take its place, the same beautiful
substance is lit up for the inmates to sit by, at their
occupations of reading, or music, or discourse. The
bee is there, with her odorous ministry. In the morning, she has probably been at the breakfast-table. In
the morning, she is honey; in the evening, the waxen
taper; in the summer noon, a voice in the garden, or
the window; in the winter, and at all other times, a
meeter of us in books. She talks Greek to us in
Sophocles and Theocritus; Virgil's very best Latin, in
his *Georgics;* we have just heard her in Italian; and
besides all her charming associations with the poets in
general, one of the Elizabethan men has made a whole
play out of her,—a play in which the whole *dramatis
personæ* are bees! And a very sweet performance it is
according to Charles Lamb, who was not lavish of his
praise. It was written by Thomas Day, one of the
fellows of Massinger and Decker, and is called the
Parliament of Bees. Lamb has given extracts from it
in his *Specimens of the Dramatic Poets,* and says in a
note :—

The doings,
The births, the wars, the wooings

of these pretty winged creatures are, with continued
liveliness, portrayed, throughout the whole of this

curious old drama, in words which bees would talk
with, could they talk; the very air seems replete
with humming and buzzing melodies while we read
them. Surely bees were never so be-rhymed before."
(Vol. ii., Moxon's latest edition, p. 130.) Would to
heaven that a horrid, heavy-headed monster called
Hepatitis—who has been hindering us from having our
way of late in the most unseasonable manner, and is at
this minute clawing our side and shoulder for our
disrespect of him—would have allowed us to go to the
British Museum, and read the whole play for ourselves.
We might have been able to give the reader some
pleasant tastes of it, besides those to be met with in
Mr. Lamb's book. The following is a specimen. Klania,
a female bee, is talking of her lovers :—

Philon, a Bee
Well skill'd in verse and amorous poetry,
As we have sate at work, *both on one rose,**
Has humm'd sweet canzons, both in verse and prose,
Which I ne'er minded. Astrophel, a Bee
 (Although not so poetical as he),
Yet in his full invention quick and ripe,
In summer evenings on his well-tuned pipe,

---

* " Prettily pilfered," says Lamb, "from the sweet passage in
the *Midsummer Night's Dream*, where Helena recounts to Hermia
their school-days' friendship: -

    ' We, Hermia, like two artificial gods,
      Created with our needles both one flower,
      Both on one sampler, sitting on one cushion.' "

Upon a woodbine blossom in the sun,
(Our hive being clean swept and our day's work done—)
Would play us twenty several tunes ; yet I
Nor minded Astrophel, nor his melody.
Then there's Amniter, for whose love fair Leade
(That pretty Bee) flies up and down the mead
With rivers in her eyes—without deserving,
Sent me trim acorn bowls of his own carving,
To drink May-dews and mead in. Yet none of these,
My hive-born playfellows and fellow Bees,
Could I affect, until this strange Bee came.

It is pretty clear, however, from this passage, that Mr. Lamb's usual exquisite judgment was seduced by the little loves and graces of these unexpected *dramatis personæ ;* for this is certainly not the way in which bees would talk. It is all human language, and unbeelike pursuits. " Rivers in her eyes " is beautifully said, but bees do not shed tears. They are no carvers of bowls ; and we have no reason to believe that they know anything of music and poetry. The bee

Who, at her flowery work doth sing,

sings like the cicada of Anacreon, with her wings. To talk as bees would talk we must divest ourselves of flesh and blood, and develop ideas modified by an untried mode of being, and by unhuman organs. We must talk as if we had membranaceous wings, a proboscis, and no knowledge of tears and smiles ; and, as to our loves,

they would be confined to the queen and the drones—
and very unloving and unpoetical work they would make
of it. The rest of us would know nothing about it. We
should love nothing but the flowers, the brooks, our
two elegant manufactures of wax and honey, and the
whole community at large—being very patriotic, but
not at all amorous—more like tasteful Amazons than
damsels of Arcadia ; ladies with swords by their sides,
and not to be *hummed* by the beau-ideals of Mr. Thomas
Day.

These same formidable weapons of the bees, their
stings, remind us of the only drawback on the pleasures
of thinking about them—their massacres of the drones.
Every year those gentlemen have to pay for their idle
and luxurious lives by one great pang of abolition.
They are all stung and swept away into nothingness !
Truly a circumstance to "give us pause," and perplex
us with our wax and honey. It seems, however, to be
the result of an irresistible impulse—some desperate
necessity of state, for want of better knowledge, or more
available powers. We are to suppose them doing it
unwillingly, with a horror of the task proportioned to
the very haste and fury in which they perform it ; as
though they wished to get it off their hands as fast as
possible, terrified and agonised at the terror and agony
which they inflict. Why they leave this tremendous

flaw in their polity—why they govern for the most part
so well, and yet have this ugly work to do in order to
make all right at the year's end, is a question which
human beings may discuss, when nations have come to
years of discretion; when they have grown wise enough,
by the help of railroads and mutual benefits, to dispense
with cuffing one another like a parcel of schoolboys.
Mankind have not yet outlived their own massacres and
revolutions long enough to have a right to be astonished
at the massacres of the bees.   What they ought to be
astonished at, is their own notion of the beehive as a
pattern of government, with this tremendous flaw in it
staring them in the face.   But we believe they have now
become sensible of the awkwardness of the analogy.
Assuredly we should find no Archbishop of Canterbury
now-a-days arguing in the style of his predecessor, in
the play of *Henry the Fifth* :—

> So work the honey bees ;
> Creatures, that, by a rule in nature, teach
> The art of order to a peopled kingdom.
> They have a king, and officers of sorts :
> Where some, like magistrates, correct at home ;
> Others, like merchants, venture trade abroad ;
> Others, like soldiers, arméd in their stings,
> Make boot upon the summer's velvet buds ;
> Which pillage they, with merry march, bring home
> To the tent-royal of their emperor ;
> Who, busied in his majesty, surveys

The singing masons building roofs of gold;
The civil citizens kneading up the honey;
The poor mechanic porters crowding in
Their heavy burdens at his narrow gate;
The sad-eyed justice, with his surly hum,
Delivering o'er to executors pale
The lazy yawning drone.

Alas! in Beedom, the archbishop himself, inasmuch as he was no wax-chandler, would have been accounted one of these same lazy, yawning drones, and delivered over to the secular arm. Bees do not teach men, nor ought they. We have some higher things among us, even than wax and honey; and though we have our flaws, too, in the art of government, and do not yet know exactly what to do with them, we hope we shall find out. Will the bees ever do that? Do they also hope it? Do they sit pondering, when the massacre is over, and think it but a bungling way of bringing their accounts right? Man, in his self-love, laughs at such a fancy. He is of opinion that no creature can think, or make progression, but himself. What right he has, from his little experience, to come to such conclusions, we know not; but he must allow, that we know as little of the conclusions of the bees. All we feel certain of is, that with bees, as with men, the good of existence outweighs the evil; that evil itself is but a rough working towards good; and that if good can

14

ultimately be better without it, there is a thing called hope, which says it may be possible. We take our planet to be very young, and our love of progression to be one of the proofs of it; and when we think of the good, and beauty, and love, and pleasure, and generosity, and nobleness of mind and imagination, in which this green and glorious world is abundant, we cannot but conclude that the love of progression is to make it still more glorious, and add it to the number of those older stars, which are probably resting from their labours, and have become heavens.

CHAPTER XII.

MISCELLANEOUS FEELINGS RESPECTING SICILY, ITS MUSIC, ITS RELIGION, AND ITS MODERN POETRY.

DANTE'S EVENING.—AVE MARIA OF BYRON.—THE SICILIAN VESPERS.—NOTHING " INFERNAL " IN NATURE.—SICILIAN MARINER'S HYMN. — INVOCATION FROM COLERIDGE. — PAGAN AND ROMAN CATHOLIC WORSHIP. — LATIN AND ITALIAN COUPLET.—WINTER'S "RATTO DI PROSERPINA."— A HINT ON ITALIAN AIRS.—BELLINI.—MELI, THE MODERN THEOCRITUS.

TIME flies, and friends must part. In closing our Blue Jar, a rosy light seems to come over it, at once beautiful and melancholy; for terminations are

14—2

farewells, and farewells remind us of evenings, and of
the divine lines of the poet :—

> Era già l' ora, che volge 'l desio
> A' naviganti, e intenerisce 'l cuore
> Lo dì ch' an detto a' dolci amici A Dio :
> E che lo nuovo peregrin d' amore
> Punge, se ode squilla di lontano,
> Che paia 'l giorno pianger che si muore.

> 'T was now the hour, when love of home melts through
> Men's hearts at sea, and longing thoughts portray
> The moment when they bade sweet friends adieu ;
> And the new pilgrim now, on his lone way,
> Thrills as he hears the distant vesper bell,
> That seems to mourn for the expiring day.

Divine, indeed, are those lines of Dante. Why
didn't he write all such, instead of employing two
volumes out of three, to show us how much less he
cared to be divine than infernal? Was it absolutely
necessary for him to have so much black ground for
his diamonds?

And another poet who took to the black, or rather
the burlesque, side of things, how could he write so
beautifully on the same theme, and resist giving us
whole poems as tender and confiding, to assist in
making the world happy? The stanza respecting the
Ave Maria is surely the best in *Don Juan* :—

> Ave Maria! blessed be the hour!
> The time, the clime, the spot where I so oft

Have felt the moment in its fullest power
Sink o'er the earth, so beautiful and soft,
While swung the deep bell in the distant tower,
Or the faint dying day-hymn stole aloft,
And not a breath *crept through the rosy air*,
And yet the forest leaves *seemed stirr'd with prayer*.

Not, we beg leave to say, that we are Roman Catholic, either in our creed or our form of worship; though we should be not a little inclined to become such, did the creed contain nothing harsher or less just than the adoration of maternity. We have been taught to be too catholic in the true sense of the word (Universal) to wish for any ultimate form of Christianity, except that which shall drop all the perplexing thorns through which it has grown, and let the odour of its flower be recognised in its spotless force without one infernal embitterment.

But it will be said that there are infernal embitterments even in the sweetest forms of things, whether we will have them or no—massacres in bee-hives, Dantes among the greatest poets, *Sicilian* Vespers. Think of those, it will be said. Think of the horrible massacre known by the name of the " Sicilian Vespers." Think of the day in your honeyed, Hyblæan island, when the same hour which

Sinks o'er the earth, so beautiful and soft,

with not a breath in its rosy air, and with the leaves of
its trees moving as if they were lips of adoring silence,
was the signal for an indiscriminate slaughter of men,
women, and children; ay, babes at the breast, and
mothers innocent as the object of vesper worship. Was
there nothing infernal in that? Is there nothing
hellish, and of everlasting embitterment in the recollection?

No. And again a loud and happy No, of everlasting sweetness.

The infernal and the everlasting bitter imply the
same things. There is nothing infernal that has a
limit; therefore there is nothing infernal in nature.
Look round, and show it if you can. Nature will have
no unlimited pain. The sufferer swoons, or dies, or
endures; but the limit comes. Death itself is but the
dissolution of compounds that have either been dis-
ordered or worn out, and therefore cannot continue
pleasantly to co-exist. Horrible was this Sicilian
massacre; horrible and mad; one of the wildest
reactions against wickedness in human history. The
French masters of the island had grown mad with
power and debauchery, and the islanders grew mad with
revenge. It was the story in little of the French
Revolution; not the Revolution of the Three Days,
truly deserving the title of Glorious for its Christian

forbearance; but the old, untaught, delirious, Robes-
pierre Revolution. Dreadful is it to think of the vesper
bell ringing to that soft worship of the mother of Jesus,
and then of thousands of daggers, at the signal,
leaping out of the bosoms of the worshippers, and
plunging into the heart of every foreigner present, man,
woman, and child. But there came an end; soon to
the body; sooner or later, to the mind. The dead were
buried; the French government in the island was
expelled, and a better brought in. The evil perished,
good came out of it; and myriads of vespers have taken
place since then, but not one like that. Yes, myriads
of vespers—a vesper every day, ever since—from the
year 1282 to this present 1848,—all gentle, all secure
from the like misery, all more or less worthy of the
beautiful description of the poet. If the massacre
called the Sicilian Vespers had been infernal, it would
have been going on now! and nature has not made
such hellish enormities possible. The only durability
to which she tends is a happy one. Her shortest lives
(generally speaking) are her least healthy; her greatest
longevities are those of healthy serenity. Supposing
the earth to be animated (as some have thought it), we
cannot conceive it to be unhappy, rolling, as it has done
for ages, round the sun, with a swiftness like the blood
in the veins of childhood. Eternity of existence is

inconceivable on any ground of analogy, except as identical with healthy prevalence; and healthy prevalence, with sensation, is inconceivable apart from sensations of pleasure.

Gone long ago are the bad Sicilian Vespers; but the good Sicilian Vespers, the beautiful Sicilian music, the beautiful Sicilian poetry, these remain; and, as if in sweet scorn of the catastrophe, they are particularly famous for their gentleness. To be told that a Sicilian air is about to be sung, is to be prepared to hear something especially sweet and soft. Every Protestant as well as Roman Catholic lover of music knows the *Sicilian Mariner's Hymn;* and is a Catholic, if not a Roman worshipper, while he sings it. Fancy it rising at a distance out of the white-sailed boat in the darkling blue waters, when the sun has just gone down, and the rock on the woody promontory above the chapel, whose bell gave the notice, is touched with rose-colour. Nay, fancy you forget all this, and think only of the honest simple mariners singing this hymn, at the moment when their wives and children are repeating the spirit of it on shore, and all Italy is doing the same:

O sanctissima, O purissima,
Dulcis Virgo Maria !
Mater amata, intemerata,
Ora pro nobis !

O most holy, O most spotless,
Mary, Virgin glorious !
Mother dearest, maiden clearest—
Oh, we pray thee, pray for us.

The sweetest of English poets could not resist echoing this kind of evening music in a strain of his own ; but though he did it in the course of an invocation, it is rather a description than a prayer. It is, however, very Sicilian :—

INVOCATION.

Sung behind the scenes in Coleridge's tragedy of " Remorse ; " to be accompanied, says the poet, by " soft music from an instrument of glass or steel."

Hear, sweet spirit—hear the spell !
Lest a blacker charm compel ;
So shall the midnight breezes swell
With thy deep long-lingering knell ; .

(Observe the various yet bell-like intonation of that last verse, and the analogous feeling in the repetition of the rhyme)

*And at evening evermore,
In a chapel on the shore,*
Shall the chanters, *sad and saintly,*
Yellow tapers burning faintly,
Doleful masses chant for thee,
Miserere, Domine !

> Hark ! the cadence dies away
> On the yellow moonlight sea :
> The boatmen rest their oars, and say,
> *Miserere, Domine !*

The tapers are yellow in the chapel, and the moonlight yellow out of doors—one of those sympathies of colour which are often finer than contrast.

Coleridge was so fond of sweet sounds, that he makes one of the characters in this play exclaim,—

> If the bad spirit retain'd his angel's voice,
> Hell scarce were hell.

The Pagans of old were of the same opinion, for they made Pluto break his inexorable laws at the sound of the harp of Orpheus, his eyes, in spite of themselves, being forced to shed " *iron* tears," as Milton finely calls them.   The notes, as the poet says,

> *Drew* iron tears down Pluto's cheek,
> And made Hell grant what Love did seek.

" The grim king of the ghosts " would not have shed them if he could have helped it.   So Moschus, in his *Elegy on the Death of Bion*, expresses his opinion that if his deceased friend would sing a pastoral to the Queen of Pluto, " something *Sicilian*," as he emphatically calls it (Σικελικόν τι), she could not have the heart to deny his return to earth.   One should like to know the hymns which the Pagans actually sung to

Proserpina and her mother Ceres, and how far they coincided, perhaps in some instances were identical, with strains now sung in the Catholic churches. Some of the oldest chants are supposed to be of Greek origin; and indeed it would be marvellous if *all* the ancient music had been swept away, considering how many ceremonies, vestments, odours, processions, churches themselves, and, to say the truth, opinions, were retained by the new creed from the old—wisely in many instances, most curiously in all. Very naturally, too; for the knees are the same knees with which all human beings kneel, Pagan or Christian; and the sky is the same to which they look up, whether inhabited by saints or goddesses. Nor is there anything " blasphemous " (as zealous Protestants are too quick to assert) in the Roman Catholic tendency to use the same kind of language towards the one, as was held and hymned towards the other; for blasphemy signifies what is injurious to the character of the divinity, and nothing is injurious to it except the attribution of injustice and cruelty. If theological opinions, of whatever creed, offended in nothing worse than an excess of zeal towards the beauty of the maternal character, or in behalf of the supposition that the spirits of the good and pious interested themselves in our welfare, the human heart would be little disposed to quarrel with

them, in times even more enlightened than the present.
There is a couplet extant in Italy, remarkable for being
both Italian and Latin.   It might have been addressed
by a Pagan of the Lower Roman Empire, to the goddess
Proserpina, when *she* was the guardian angel of Sicily,
or to the Virgin Mary, by a modern Roman Catholic;
and we find nothing horrible in this.   On the contrary,
it seems to fuse the two eras gently and tenderly
together, by the same affecting link of human want
and natural devotion.   This is the couplet :—

> In mare irato, in subita procella,
> Invoco te, nostra benigna stella.

> In sudden storms, and when the billows blind,
> Thee I invoke, star sweet to human kind!

When we spoke, in a former chapter, of the
beautiful Sicilian story of Proserpina, we forgot (a very
ungrateful piece of forgetfulness) to add, that one of the
loveliest tributes ever paid to it by genius, is the
Ratto di Proserpina—Winter's opera so called.   There
is every charm of the subject in it,—the awfulness of
the greater gods, the genial maternity of Ceres, the
tender memory of her daughter, the cordial re-assurances
given her by Mercury, the golden-age dances of the
shepherds.   What smile of encouragement ever surpassed that of the strain on the words *Cerere tornerà*,
in the divine trio, *Mi lasci, O madre amata?*   What

passionate mixture of delight and melancholy, the world-famous duet of *Vaghi colli?* Why does not some publisher make an *Elegant Extracts* of such music from composers that will survive all fashion, and have comments written upon them, like those on poets? What would we not give to see such an edition of the finest airs of all the great inventive melodists, the Pergoleses and Paisiellos and their satellites, and all the inventive harmonists too, the Bachs, Corellis, and Beethovens, each with *variorum* notes from the best critics, and loving indications of the beauties of particular passages? Publications of this kind are yet wanting, to the honour, and glory, and thorough household companionship of the art of music: and it is a pity somebody does not take the opportunity of setting about them, when there are critics, both in and out of the profession, qualified to do them justice.*

We cannot close our Jar better than with a taste of "the modern Theocritus," Giovanni Meli, who deserves his title, and whose very name, as we said before, signifies honey. *Meli* is honey, both in modern Sicilian and in ancient Greek; and the poet

---

* Why does not Mr. Edward Holmes do it? or Mr. Chorley? We have heard that M. Berlioz has some such work in hand, with a translation of which his friends are to favour the public. Such a production, if copious, might form an epoch in the critical history of the art. We hope a time will come when music will be as freely quoted in books as poetry is.

may be a descendant of the Greek possessors of the
island; nay (to carry the fancy out), possibly of
Theocritus himself! Who is to prove, on the beautiful negative principle, that he was not?

Meli was an abbate at Palermo, a doctor of medicine, public professor of chemistry in the University
there, and member of several academies. So are his
titles set forth in the edition of his poems in seven
volumes, which we have had the pleasure, since these
chapters were first written, of picking up at a book-
stall in Holborn. They are not very pastoral-sounding
titles; yet the more knowledge the better, even for
the shepherd; and the shepherd-poet turns it all to
account, just as chemistry itself improves the field and
the flowers. One of the friends whom Theocritus
himself has immortalised, was a physician. We have
it on the authority of a gentleman who knew the
Abbate Meli, that he was as good a man as he was a
charming poet. He seemed to live only (he says) to
do good and to give pleasure : and he was as much
beloved by the poor, as his company was in request
among the prosperous. To say that Meli was to be of
the party, was to give an evening assembly of friends
its highest zest. His virtues were anything but
narrow. He was temperate, but not ascetic. He
balked no genial inspiration: was a modern Anacreon

as well as Theocritus ; evinced a liberal turn of mind
in every respect, without offence; and could write
hymns full of natural piety, as well as drinking and
love songs. He was also a deeply read man, and a
solid thinker. One of his longest poems is a banter
upon the various assumptions of philosophy respecting
the system of the world. Heartily do we wish it were
in our power to give as good an account of the poems
as of their titles ; but though they have a glossary for
the benefit of " the Italians," we cannot yet boast
such a knowledge of them as qualifies us to say much
in evidence, beyond their general merits. These we
can discern well enough, like glimmerings of nymphs
and flocks among the trees ; and very like Theocritus
indeed is his genius ; very true to nature and to
manners, impulsive in its style, not afraid of collo-
quialisms and homely traits, but with an air of grace
over all, and the right happy aroma of the subtle and
the suggestive. The moment you open his first
eclogue, you meet with a picture truly Theocritan. A
herdsman asks a shepherdess if she has seen a cow of
his which is missing, and he thus accosts her :—

> O Pasturedda, di li trizzi ad unna,
> Chi fai pinnata di la manu manca,
> Pri' un t' appighiari ssa facciuzza biunna.

" O shepherdess with the waving locks, who make a

penthouse over your eyes with your left hand, for fear of embrowning your pretty face," &c.

Meli was poor, till, doubtless, he thought himself rich on receiving a small pension from the late King Ferdinand; for which (says the author of an interesting article on the "Dialects and Literature of Southern Italy," in the *British Quarterly Review*) " the poet expressed his gratitude in respectful, but not adulatory terms."

The dialect of Sicily is remarkable for preferring close sounds to broad ones. It converts the Tuscan *l*'s into *d*'s, and its *e*'s and *o*'s into *i*'s and *u*'s. Thus, "bella" becomes *bedda*; "padre," *patri*; "mare," *mari*; " sono," *sunnu*; "colorito," *culuritu*, &c. This is reversing the state of things in the days of Theocritus, when the Dorian inhabitants of Sicily were accused of doing nothing when they spoke but " yawn " and " gabble."* But it is attributed to the Arabs, when they were masters of the island. It has, probably, been injurious to the cause of music, and hindered the Sicilians from producing as many fine composers as their Neapolitan neighbours. Thus much, lest the reader should start at the strange, though pretty, look of Meli's Italian, the poet having

---

* See a pleasant allusion to this charge by Theocritus himself, at page 84 of the present book, where Praxinoe disburses a quantity of *a*'s.

wisely chosen to speak in the tongue of those, from whose natures and homes he copied.

The reader will see at once this leading difference between the Italian language and the Sicilian form of it, in the following opening stanzas of one of Meli's canzonets, accompanied by a Tuscan version from the pen of Professor Rosini :—

Sti silenzii, sta virdura,	Questa ombrifera verdura,
Sti muntagni, sti vallati,	Queste tacite vallate,
L' ha criatu la Natura	L' ha create la Natura
Pri li cori innamurati.	Sol per l' alme innamorate.
Lu susurru di li frunni,	Il susurro delle fronde,
Di li sciumi lu lamentu,	Del rio garrulo il lamento,
L' aria, l' ecu chi rispunni,	L' aria, l' eco che risponde,
Tuttu spira sentimentu.	Tutto spira sentimento.

" These quiet and green places, these mountains and valleys, were created by Nature on purpose for loving hearts.

" The whispering of the leaves, the murmuring of the waters, the falling and rising of the wind—everything inspires the innermost feelings."

So, in the beginning of Eclogue the Second, a countryman, who seems fatigued, accosts another who is sitting at his door, and asks him whether his dogs are gentle, and he may venture to come in. The good householder begs him to stand a minute or two on the rock-stone, and he will call the dogs off.

"Come here, Scamper," says he, "*thumping the
ground there with your tail.*   Quiet, Wasp, quiet!
Down, Lion! Now you can come in, and rest yourself; and I hope you'll stop and take something. I
have a new cheese at your service, and a piping hot
loaf, just out of the oven, made of capital bread," &c.

The graphic animation of this exordium, particularly the passage we have marked in Italics, is quite
in the spirit of Theocritus. But we are obliged to
stop short in it for want of understanding the next
sentence.

Theocritus could satirize a king. In the following
passage in his *Winter Idyll*, Meli is perhaps covertly
sticking his sly pen into a monk. A good old grand-
sire is proposing to have what we should now call a
Christmas dinner; and he consults his family as to
what shall be the principal dish—what meat he shall
kill:—

> Ora è lu tempu,
> Ch'unu di li domestici animali
> Mora pri nui; ma mi dirriti: quali?
> Lu voi, la vacca, l'*asinu*, la crapa
> Sù stati sempri a parti tuttu l'annu
> Di li nostri travagghi; e na gran parti
> Duvemu an iddi di li nostri beni;
> Vi pari, chi sarria riconoscenza
> Digna di nui, na tali ricompenza?
>
> Ma lu porcu? lu porcu è statu chiddu,
> Chi a li travagghi d' autri ed a li nostri

E statu un ozziusu spettaturi ;
Anzi abbusannu di li nostri curi ;
Mai s' è dignatu scotiri lu ciancu
Da lu fangusu lettu, a proprii pedi
Aspittannu lu cibbu, e cu arroganza
Nui sgrida di l' insolita tardanza.
Chistu, chi nun conusci di la vita,
Chi li suli vantaggi, e all' autri lassa
Li vuccuni chiù amari, comu tutti
Fussimu nati pri li soi piaciri ;
Chi immersu tra la vili sua pigrizzia
Stirannusi da l' unu e l' autru latu
Di li suduri d' autru s' è ingrassatu ;
Si : chistu mora, e ingrassi a nui : lu porcu,
Lu vili, lu putruni —
Si : l' ingrassatu a costu d' autru, mora.

Lettu già lu prucessu ; e proferuta,
   Fra lu comuni applausu e la gioja,
   La fatali sintenza ; attapanciatu,
   Strascinatu, attacatu, stramazzatu
   Fù lu porcu a l' istanti ; un gran cuteddu
   Sprofundannusi dintra di la gula,
   Ci ricerca lu cori, e ci disciogghi
   Lu gruppu di la vita : orrendi grida,
   Gemiti strepitusi, aria ed oricchi
   Sfardanu e a li vicini, e a li luntani,
   Ed anchi fannu sentiri a li stiddi
   La grata nova di lu gran maceddu.
   Saziu già di la straggi lu cuteddu
   Apri niscennu, spaziusa strata
   A lu sangu, ed a l' anima purcina ;
   L' unu cadennu dintra lu tineddu,
   Prometti sangunazzi ; e l' autra scappa,
   E si disperdi in aria tra li venti,

O com' è fama, passa ad abitari
Dintru lu corpu di un riccuni avaru,
Giacchì nun potti in terra ritruvari
Chiù vili e schiufusu munnizzaru.

"The bull, cow, *donkey*, and goat have all shared
in the labours of the year, and assisted to keep us ; so
that to slaughter one of those would hardly be grateful. But the pig ! What think you of the pig ? *He*
has been nothing but a lazy spectator—a fellow living
on those labours ; nay, an abuser of the care we take
to keep him ; for he scorns to stir from his muddy
bed, expects his food to be laid at his feet, and even
has the arrogance to cry out against us if we are not
in a hurry. Nothing of life knows he but its luxuries ;
he leaves all his cares to us, as if we were born for
nothing else but to heap him with enjoyments.
Plunged in the vilest indolence, he contents himself
with turning from one side to the other, and growing
fat with the sweat of our brows. Oh, he must die by
all means, and fatten us in our turn. The hog—the
vile wretch—the poltroon—the corpulent selfish rascal
—Death to him !

"No sooner said than done. The sentence is
carried by acclamation. The pig is grappled with,
dragged along, tied and bound, slain utterly, through
and through. The huge knife, profoundly plunged

into that gullet of his, goes to his heart amid horrid
shrieks and dinning lamentations, which bear the
news of the great deed to friends afar off, and to the
very stars in heaven. Blood and soul, in a flood
ample as the way made for them, follow the with-
drawing blade,—*l' anima purcina*, the spirit of pork;
the blood into a hogshead, promising black puddings;
the soul, either into the passing winds, or, as others
think, into the body of some greedy chuff of a million-
aire, that vilest and most repulsive of muck-worms."

Meli's first volume consists entirely of bucolics;
the second of odes, sonnets, and canzonets; the third
chiefly of verses in the manner of Berni, of satires,
and dithyrambics; the fourth is occupied with a long
Bernesque poem, called the *Fairy Galanta*, seemingly
full of national as well as critical matters; the fifth and
sixth with another on Don Quixote; and the seventh
with elegies and fables. By this the reader may judge
of the diversity of his genius, and its tendency to the
sprightly; with which, however, a fund of thinking is
always mixed up. He was evidently forced to conceal a
great deal of deep thought and indignant sympathy in
the garb of a jester. He did this, however, so well, expressed so much horror at the French revolution, and
showed himself such a friend of all who had anything
good in them, that in a country notorious for its arbi-

trary government, he was in favour with the court and
aristocracy; and the circumstance, upon the whole,
does them credit. Princes in Sicily are as common as
country squires in England; but they have beautiful
titles, and it is pleasant to read the list of his subscribers. Among them, here and there, is the name
of an Englishman ludicrously set forth. Thus we
have *Sua Altezza Reale*, &c., to wit :—

His Royal Highness Prince Don Leopoldo Borbone—A
hundred copies.
His Excellency the Signor Prince della Trabia---Ten copies.
Her Excellency the Signora Princess della Trabia.
The Most Illustrious Signor Marquis Cardillo—A hundred
copies.
Mister Becker (probably Baker)—Two copies.
My Lord the Great Chamberlain Don Gasparo Leone.
The Most Illustrious Signor Duke di Campobello.
Don Francesco Orlando.
Don Antonino Sirretta.
Don Giuseppe *Benthilley* (probably Mr. Joseph Bentley).
Don Giuseppe Romano.
Lieutenant-Colonel Don Filippo Cellano.
The Most Illustrious Marquis della Gran Montagna.
Don Antonino Lucchese Pepoli.
Her Excellency the Signora Princess of Pandolfina. (What
a noble word !)
The Most Illustrious Marquis of Altavilla.
Her Excellency the Signora Princess of Paternò.
Her Excellency the Signora Duchess della Grazia.
Don Michèle *Beaumont*.
His Excellency the Reverend Lord Gravina, Bishop of
Flaviopolis.

The Most Illustrious Count Don Giuseppe de Monroy, of
    the Princes of Pandolfina.
His Excellency the Signor Prince of Villafranca.
The Most Illustrious Prince of Villadorata.
The Most Illustrious Don Vincenzo Jacona di Catania,
    Baron of Castellana.

But we shall never have done playing this beautiful
tune of a nomenclature.

The most agreeable specimen of Meli remains to be
given. It is done to our hand by the reviewer before
mentioned; and is done so well, that we are spared the
difficulty of attempting it after him. We therefore
give it in his own prose version. It luckily happens to
be one that furnishes direct comparison with Meli's prototype, and with the Latin and English followers of that
original. Most readers of Pope will recollect a passage
in which he describes a coquettish girl, who attracts
her lover's attention while pretending not to do so.
But see how the natural thoughts originally suggested
by Theocritus are subjected to the artificial manner.
The principal idea you have, is not of the things, but of
the words, and of their classical construction :—

STREPHON.   Me gentle *Delia* beckons *from the plain*,
             Then, hid in shades, *eludes* her eager *swain ;*
             But *feigns a laugh,* to see me search around,
             And by that laugh *the willing fair* is found.

DAPHNIS. The sprightly *Sylvia* trips along the green :
　　　　　She *runs*, but hopes she *does not run* unseen :
　　　　　While a kind glance at her pursuer flies,
　　　　　How much at variance are her feet and eyes !
　　　　　　　　　　　　　—POPE's *Pastorals.*

Very epigrammatic that, and as unlike pastoral as
the ball-rooms could desire !   It was a horrible spoiling
of Virgil :—

　　　Malo me Galatea petit, lasciva puella,
　　　Et fugit ad salices, et se cupit ante videri.
　　　　　　　　　　—*Eclog.* iii. v. 64.

Thus translated by Dryden :—

　　　My Phillis me with pelted apples plies ;
　　　Then tripping to the woods the wanton hies,
　　　And wishes to be seen before she flies.

The Latin poet, too, in the flight of the damsel,
added a charming idea to the one suggested by Theocritus ; if, indeed, the Greek did not give the first hint
of it himself—

　　　Βάλλει καὶ μαλοῖσι τὸν αἰπόλον ἁ Κλεάριστα,
　　　Τὰς αἶγας παρέλευντα, καὶ ἁδύ τι ποππυλιάσδει.
　　　　　　　　　　—*Idyll* v., v. 88.

Literally, " Clearista pelts the goatherd with apples, as
he goes by with his goats, and then hums something
sweet."

The goatherd here does not seem to stop.   It is not
certain that he and the damsel are acquainted ; though

he wishes to imply that she loves him. In case they are intimate, we are to suppose that she intends him to imagine her saying something very pleasant, though he is too far off to hear it; but in the other case, Virgil probably understood her to pretend that she had not pelted the apples at all; for which reason she falls to humming a tune, with an air of innocent indifference.

Be this as it may, nobody will deny the truly natural and Theocritan style in which the modern Sicilian has enlarged upon the old suggestion.

" Meli," says the reviewer, " introduces a group of fishing-girls, chattering and joking, and telling of their loves, in the absence of their parents. Their very names, Pidda, Lidda, and Ridda, sound congenial to their condition. To an invitation to go and romp on the sands, Lidda prudishly replies that she is afraid of meeting some rude swain. Ridda also tells a story of having seen a fisherman concealed behind the rocks, who addresses her in an amorous song, which frightened her out of her senses. But Pidda, who is the eldest of the three, loses patience at this affected simplicity, and exclaims—

> Eh via—muzzica ccâ stu jiditeddu ;
> E vaja franca, ca nni canuscemu ;
> Avemu tutti lu 'nnamurateddu.

Literally,—' Come, poor innocents, bite my little

finger; but let that pass; we know each other, and that each of us has her sweetheart.'

"Lidda, at last, casts off her shyness, and sings the following pretty ditty—

> Quannu a Culicchia jeu vogghiu parrari,
>   Ca spissu spissu mi veni lu sfilu,
> A la finestra mi mettu a filari ;
>   Quann' iddu passa, poi rumpu lu filu ;
> Cadi lu fusu ; ed eu mettu a gridari,
>   ' Gnuri, pri carità proitimilu.'
> Iddu lu pigghia ; mi metti a guardari ;
> Jeu mi uni vaju suppilu suppilu.

"When I wish to speak to my sweetheart, which occurs pretty often, I seat myself at the window to spin ; and when he is passing underneath, I manage to break the thread ; the spindle falls (out of the window), and I cry out, dolefully, ' Oh, friend, be so kind as to pick it up for me ! ' He does so, and looks at me, when I feel out of my wits for joy."

We shall not close our Jar with anything less good than this. There are still, indeed, divers good things of ancient Sicilian poetry—one or two in particular —which we are wrong not to have given the English reader some taste of (as far as we could), while writing our chapters on them ; and also some passages from modern travellers, which, as illustrating other points of our subject, we think would have been found welcome by the reader. These, therefore, we have put by themselves in the following pages, under a title which shows them to have been part of our stock; and so, submitting them to his judgment, conclude by wishing both him and his all the good things in the world.

OVERFLOWINGS OF THE JAR.

THE JOURNEY TO THE FEAST.

(FROM THEOCRITUS.)

THIS, instead of an "overflowing," ought to have been a constituent part of the Jar, because it supplies what has been wanting to complete our specimens of Theocritus; namely, a sample of the happiest and most enjoying portion of his genius. The original is one of his finest productions. The chief part of it relates what befell him on his way to a friend's house out of town, to join a party at harvest-home. He overtakes a brother poet, who, in respect to his condition in life, might have been to Theocritus what a Burns from the plough might have been to a "gentleman," had any such rival poet existed in Burns' time. This inspired rustic, who (with the propriety noticed in our remarks on the subject) speaks as well as the gentleman himself, is represented as reciting a poem of his composition, to beguile the

way. Theocritus, in return, recites a composition of
his own ; and the whole piece concludes with a description of the luxurious orchard nest which awaited our
author on his arrival at the house he was going to :—

Once on a time myself and Eucritus
Went out of town, taking Amyntas with us,
To join a feast of Ceres, that was given
By Phrasidâmus and Antigenes,
Sons of Lycòpeus, and descended too
(If that is anything) from Clitias,
Ay, and from Calcon, who with his strong foot
Dug from the rock the fount there, at Burinna,
Where you perceive such a thick bower of elms
And poplars, making quite a roof o'erhead.

We had not got half way, nor yet discern'd
The tomb of Brasilas, when we overtook,
Travelling along, a favourite of the Muse,—
A goatherd, of the name of Lycidas ;
And goatherd well he seem'd ; for on his shoulders
Hung a right simple goatskin, hairy and thick,
Smelling as if 'twas new ; about his body
Was an old jerkin, tied with platted straw ;
And in his hand he bore a crooked stick
Made of wild olive. Placidly he turned,
A little smile parting his kindly lips,
And with a genial eye accosting me,
Said, " Ah, Theocritus ! and where go you
At noon, when all the lizards are asleep,
And not a lark but sobers ? Is't a feast
You're making haste to, or some vintager's,
That thus you dash the pebbles with your sandals ? "

" Lycidas," answered I, " the world, my friend,
Shepherds, reapers, and all, count you a poet
Of the first pastoral order,—which delights me :
Nevertheless, I hope you see another.
It *is* a feast we're going to. Some friends
Keep one to-day to holy Mother Earth,
For gratitude, their garners are so full.
But come ;—as we are going the same way,
And love the same good pastime, let's indulge
Each other's vein a little ; for my lips
Breathe also of the Muse ; and people call me
Greatest of living song ;—a praise, however,
Of which I am not credulous,—no, by Earth ;
For there's Philetas, and our Samian too,
Whom I no more pretend to have surpass'd,
Than frogs the grasshoppers."

        Well ;—we agreed ;
And Lycidas, with one of his sweet smiles,
Said, " You must let me give you, when we finish,
This olive-stick, for you have proved yourself
A scion truly from the stock of Jove.
I also hate the builder that pretends
To rival mountain-tops, and just as much
Those dunghill cocks that tear their throats in vain
With trying to outcrow Homer himself !
But come, let us begin, Theocritus.—
Well,—I'll be first then. Tell me if you like
This little piece, friend, which I hammered out
The other day as I was pacing Ætna."

Lycidas here commences his recitation of the following verses, which are in honour of a friend who has
gone abroad, and include the Legend of Comatas :—

" Ageanax, if he forgets me not
His faithful friend, shall safely cross the seas
To Mitylene, both when the south wind,
Warned by the westering Kids,* adds wet to wet,
And when Orion dips his sparkling feet.
Let halcyons smooth the billows, and make still
The west wind and the fiercer east, which stirs
The lowest sea-weeds ;—halcyons, of all birds
Dear to the blue-eyed Nymphs, and fed by them.
Let all things favour the kind voyager,
And land him safely ;—and that day, will I,
Wearing a crown of roses or white violets,
Quaff by my fireside Pteleatic wine ;
And some one shall dress beans ; and I will have
A noble couch, to lie at ease upon,
Heaped up of asphodel and yielding herbs ;
And there I'll drink in a divine repose,
Calling to mind Ageanax, and drain
With clinging lips the goblet to the dregs :
And there shall be two shepherds to play to me
Upon the pipe ; and Tityrus, standing by,
Shall sing how Daphnis was in love with Xenia,
And used to walk the Mountain, while the oaks
Moaned to him on the banks of Himera ;
And how he melted in his love away,
Like snows on Athos, or on Rhodope,
Or Hæmus, or the farthest Caucasus ;—
And Tityrus shall sing also, how of old
The goatherd by his cruel lord was bound,
And left to die in a great chest ; and how
The busy bees, up coming from the meadows
To the sweet cedar, fed him with soft flowers,
Because the Muse had filled his mouth with nectar.

---

* The constellation so called.

Yes, all those sweets were thine, blessed Comatas
And thou wast put into the chest, and fed
By the blithe bees, and passed a pleasant time.
Would that in my time also thou wert living,
That we might keep our flocks upon the Mountain,
And I might hear thy voice, while thou shouldst lie
Under the oak-trees or the pines, and modulate
Thy pipe deliciously, divine Comatas."

Here ended he his song, and thus in turn
I took up mine :—" Dear Lycidas, the Nymphs
Have taught me also, while I kept my flocks,
Excellent subjects ; and the best of all
I'll tell you now, since you are dear to them."

Theocritus here commences his recitation in turn,
the subject of which is an unsuccessful passion of his
friend Aratus, supposed to be the contemporary poet of
that name, author of the *Phænomena :—*

" — 'Twas on the unlucky side the Loves sneezed to me,
For I love Myrto, as the goats love spring,
But to no purpose.   Meanwhile too, Aratus,
My best of friends, becomes in love with Pholoe.
Aristis has long known it,—good Aristis,
To whom Apollo's self would not disdain
To play his harp from his own golden seat.—
O Pan, who gained by lot the lovely grounds
Of Homole,—Oh, send her to his arms,
Her, or another girl as beautiful !
Oh, do but so, and the Arcadian youth
Shall scourge thee not with squills, when they have miss'd
Their hunted game :—but if thou dost it not,
Thou shalt be flayed, and sent to sleep in straw :
In mountains and by rivers of the north

16

Mid winter shalt thou pass ; and then in summer
Be changed to utmost Æthiopia, there
To tend thy flocks under the Blemyan rock,
Where thou canst see not Nile.*—But you, ye Loves,
With your sweet apple cheeks, leave the moist nooks
Of Hyetis and Byblis and fly up
To Venus's own heaven, and thence, ah thence,
Shoot with your arrows for me this desir'd one,
Shoot,—since she pities not my friend and guest.
Riper is she than the moist pear ; and yet
The women say to her, ' Alas, alas,
Your flower will wither, Pholoe, on the stalk ! '
Come then, Aratus ; let us lie no more
At these proud doors, nor wear our feet with journeys ;
But let another, if he chooses, start
With sleepless eyes to hear the crowing cock ;
And leave such labours to the wrestler Molon.
Care we for nought but comfort : let us seek
Some ancient dame, who, muttering o'er a charm,
Shall keep away from us all things unkindly."

I ended ; and with one of his old smiles,
He gave me his poetic gift, the olive-stick ;
And turning to the left, struck off for Pyxa.
We then went on to Phrasidamus's,—
Eucritus, I, and the good little Amyntas,—
And gladly rested upon deep thick couches
Of lentisk, and of vine-leaves freshly cut.
Above our heads a throng of elms and poplars
Kept stirring ; and from out a cave o' the Nymphs
A sacred runnel, pouring forth, ran gurgling.

* This sample, strange as it may appear, of the familiarity which breeds contempt, even towards objects of worship, and which Theocritus must have smiled while he was describing, has not been confined to Paganism.

Hot in the greenest leaves, labour'd away
Those chatterers the cicadas ; the sad tree-frog
Kept his good distance in the thorny bush ;
The larks and linnets sang ; the stock-dove mourned ;
And round the fountain spun the yellow bees :
All things smelt rich of summer, rich of autumn :
Pears were about our feet, and by our side
Apples on apples roll'd ; the boughs bent down
To the very earth with loads of damson plums ;
And from the casks of wine of four years old,
We broke the corking pitch.—O ye who keep
Parnassus' top, ye Nymphs of Castaly,
Did ever Chiron, in the rocky cave
Of Pholos, set such goblets before Hercules ?
Did ever that old shepherd of Anapus,
Great Polyphemus, who could throw the rocks,
Compose such nectar to go dance withal,—
As on that day ye broached for us, O Nymphs,
Before the altar of Earth's generous Mother ?
Oh, may I riot in her heaps again
With a great winnow ; while she stands and smiles,
Holding, in either hand, poppies and wheat.

ELEGY ON THE DEATH OF BION.

(FROM MOSCHUS.)

THE chief characteristic both of this Sicilian poet Moschus and his friend Bion was a tender and elegant sweetness. We have endeavoured to modulate our version accordingly.

This is the pastoral poetry of books, as distinguished from that of real life; yet it has a real echo in the minds of those who can pass from one region to the other; nor is it wanting in some touches exquisitely human, as we have seen in the famous passage already quoted from the Elegy respecting the (supposed) difference between the transitory nature of man and the rejuvenescence of flowers :—

> Moan with me, moan, ye woods and Dorian waters,
> And weep, ye rivers, the delightful Bion;
> Ye plants, now stand in tears; murmur, ye groves;
> Ye flowers, sigh forth your odours with sad buds;
> Flush deep, ye roses and anemones;
> And more than ever now, O hyacinth, show
> Your written sorrows; *—the sweet singer's dead.

> Raise, raise the dirge, Muses of Sicily.
> Ye nightingales, that mourn in the thick leaves,
> Tell the Sicilian streams of Arethuse,
> Bion the shepherd's dead; and that with him
> Melody's dead, and gone the Dorian song.

> Raise, raise the dirge, Muses of Sicily.
> Weep on the waters, ye Strymonian swans,
> And utter forth a melancholy song,
> Tender as his whose voice was like your own;
> And say to the Œagrian girls, and say
> To all the nymphs haunting in Bistony,
> The Doric Orpheus is departed from us.

---

* Alluding to the letters AI, which simply signifies " Alas," and which are to be found (so to speak) in the dark lines or specks observable in the petals of the Turk's-cap Lily; which Professor Martyn has shown to be the true hyacinth of the ancients.

Raise, raise the dirge, Muses of Sicily.
No longer pipes he to the charmed herds,
No longer sits under the lonely oaks,
And sings ; but to the ears of Pluto now
Tunes his Lethean verse ; and so the hills
Are voiceless ; and the cows that follow still
Beside the bulls, low and will not be fed.

Raise, raise the dirge, Muses of Sicily.
Apollo, Bion, wept thy sudden fate :
The Satyrs too, and the Priapuses
Dark-veiled, and for that song of thine the Pans,
Groan'd ; and the fountain-nymphs within the woods
Mourn'd for thee, melting into tearful waters ;
Echo too mourn'd among the rocks that she
Must hush —and imitate thy lips no longer ;
Trees and the flowers put off their loveliness ;
Milk flows not as 'twas used ; and in the hive
The honey moulders,—for there is no need,
Now that thy honey's gone, to look for more.

Raise, raise the dirge, Muses of Sicily.
Not so the dolphins mourn'd by the salt sea,
Not so the nightingale among the rocks,
Not so the swallow over the far downs,
Not so Ceyx called for his Halcyone,
Not so in the eastern valleys Memnon's bird
Scream'd o'er his sepulchre for the Morning's son,
As all have mourned for the departed Bion.

Raise, raise the dirge, Muses of Sicily.
Ye nightingales and swallows every one
Whom he once charm'd and taught to sing at will
Plain to each other midst the green tree boughs
With other birds o'erhead.   Mourn too, ye doves.

Raise, raise the dirge, Muses of Sicily.
Who now shall play thy pipe, O most desir'd one!
Who lay his lip against thy reeds? who dare it?
For still they breathe of thee and of thy mouth,
And Echo comes to seek her voices there.
Pan's be they; and ev'n he shall fear perhaps
To sound them, lest he be not first hereafter.

Raise, raise the dirge, Muses of Sicily.
And Galatea weeps, who loved to hear thee,
Sitting beside thee on the calm sea-shore;
For thou didst play far better than the Cyclops,
And him the fair one shunn'd: but thee, but thee,
She used to look at sweetly from the water.
But now forgetful of the deep, she sits
On the lone sands, and feeds thy herd for thee.

Raise, raise the dirge, Muses of Sicily.
The Muse's gifts all died with thee, O shepherd,
Men's admiration, and sweet women's kisses.
The Loves about thy sepulchre weep sadly,
For Venus loved thee, much more than the kiss
With which of late she kiss'd Adonis, dying.
Thou too, O Meles, sweetest-voiced of rivers,
Thou too hast undergone a second grief;
For Homer first, that sweet mouth of Calliope,
Was taken from thee; and they say thou mournedst
For thy great son with many-sobbing streams,
Filling the far-seen ocean with a voice.
And now, again, thou weepest for a son,
Melting away in misery. Both of them
Were favourites of the fountain-nymphs; one drank
The Pegasean fount, and one his cup
Fill'd out of Arethuse; the former sang
The bright Tyndarid lass, and the great son

Of Thetis, and Atrides Menelaus;
But he, the other, not of wars or tears
Told us, but intermix'd the pipe he play'd
With songs of herds, and as he sung he fed them;
And he made pipes, and milk'd the gentle heifer,
And taught us how to kiss, and cherish'd love
Within his bosom, and was worthy of Venus.

Raise, raise the dirge, Muses of Sicily.
Every renowned city and every town
Mourns for thee, Bion;—Ascra weeps thee more
Than her own Hesiod; the Bœotian woods
Ask not for Pindar so; nor patriot Lesbos
For her Alcæus; nor th' Ægean isle
Her poet; nor does Paros so wish back
Archilochus; and Mitylene now,
Instead of Sappho's verses, rings with thine.
All the sweet pastoral poets weep for thee,—
Sicelidas the Samian; Lycidas,
Who used to look so happy; and at Cos,
Philetas; and at Syracuse, Theocritus;
All in their several dialects: and I,
I too, no stranger to the pastoral song,
Sing thee a dirge Ausonian, such as thou
Taughtest thy scholars, honouring us as all
Heirs of the Dorian Muse. Thou didst bequeath
Thy store to others, but to me thy song.

Raise, raise the dirge, Muses of Sicily.
Alas, when mallows in the garden die,
Green parsley, or the crisp luxuriant dill,
They live again, and flower another year;
But we, how great soe'er, or strong, or wise,
When once we die, sleep in the senseless earth
A long, an endless, unawakeable sleep.

Thou too in earth must be laid silently :
But the nymphs please to let the frog sing on ;
Nor envy I, for what he sings is worthless.

Raise, raise the dirge, Muses of Sicily.
There came, O Bion, poison to thy mouth,
Thou didst feel poison ; how could it approach
Those lips of thine, and not be turn'd to sweet!
Who could be so delightless as to mix it,
Or bid be mix'd, and turn him from thy song !

Raise, raise the dirge, Muses of Sicily.
But justice reaches all ;—and thus, meanwhile,
I weep thy fate. And would I could descend
Like Orpheus to the shades, or like Ulysses,
Or Hercules before him : I would go
To Pluto's house, and see if you sang there,
And hark to what you sang. Play to Prosèrpina
Something Sicilian, some delightful pastoral,
For she once play'd on the Sicilian shores,
The shores of Ætna, and sang Dorian songs,
And so thou wouldst be honour'd ; and as Orpheus
For his sweet harping, had his love again,
She would restore thee to our mountains, Bion.
Oh, had I but the power, I, I would do it.

THE SHIP OF HIERO.

" WE find an ample but interesting description, in Athenæus,
of a magnificent and prodigious galley, that had twenty benches
of rowers, contained an extraordinary number of persons, and
was not only provided with dreadful means of assault, but with

all that could delight the mind, and charm the sense. Baths of bronze and of Taurominian marble, stables, a gymnasium, small gardens planted with various trees and watered by pipes, the twining vine and ivy, a library, and a sun-dial, were all in this galley. It had three decks; the second of which was inlaid with variegated mosaic-work, containing the whole history of Homer's *Iliad*. Every necessary for repose by night, and banqueting by day, was provided with a regal luxury.

"As much timber was brought from the forest of Ætna, for the building of this galley, as would have sufficed for sixty ordinary galleys. It had three masts; and, on the upper deck, it was fortified round with a wall, and eight towers like a citadel. Each of the towers contained four combatants, completely armed, and two archers. Within, the towers were provided with missiles and stones, and on the walls stood a kind of artillery-machine, invented by Archimedes, which threw stones of three hundred-weight, and a lance twelve ells in length, to the distance of a stadium, or six hundred feet.

"Each side of the wall was provided with sixty young men, well armed; and there were shooters even in the mast-cages.* Round the upper deck was an iron rim; where there were machines placed which would act immediately against an enemy's ship, hold it fast, and draw it to the galley. A tree sufficiently large for the mainmast was long sought for in vain, till a hog-driver found one in *Brettia*, or *Bruttium*, the present South Calabria. The lower deck could be pumped by a single man, with the aid of a machine which the Greeks called κοχλίον, the Latins *cochlea*, and which we, after its inventor, name the screw of Archimedes.

"When the wonderful work was completed, it was discovered that some of the havens of Hiero would not contain it, and that in others it was not safe. Hiero therefore sent

---

* Similar perhaps to the Top, or Round-top, of a man-of-war.— *Note by the Translator.*

the galley to King Ptolemy (Ptolomæus Philadelphus, I suppose), as a present, to Alexandria.

"You will pardon me this borrowed but abbreviated description, taken from Athenæus, as it appears to me not only interesting in itself, but usefully instructive to those who have formed no just idea of the mechanics of the ancients. To such persons, I recommend the chapter in Athenæus which contains this description, as well as others, in which greater ships of the Ptolemies are described; and of one which was built by Ptolomæus Philopater, that, rowers and warriors included, could contain seven thousand men."—STOLBERG'S *Travels through Germany, Switzerland, Italy, and Sicily* (translated by HOLCROFT), vol. iv. p. 177.

SERENADES IN SICILY AND NAPLES.

"WE reached Alcamo in the evening; a well-built town, that contains above 8,000 inhabitants. It was built in the year 828, on the fruitful hill *Bonifacio*, by the Saracen *Adalcamo*, or *Halcamo*, who came from Africa; but its site was removed by the Emperor Frederick the Second to the plain in which it now stands.

"Alcamo boasts of having produced famous men; and, among others, *Ciullo del Camo*, who is generally called *Vincentio di Alcamo*. He was the contemporary of Frederick the Second, and is supposed by some to be the first who wrote poetry in the Italian language; at least, he was one of the first Italian poets. As it was Sunday, we were not surprised to see a great part of the inhabitants tumultuously crowding the streets, for this is a custom through all Italy. They begin on the Saturday evening, after the labour of the week is over, to collect in the market-places and streets. He who should be

unacquainted with their manners, would imagine that some
extraordinary event or insurrection had caused them to
assemble ; for they usually speak all together, with loud voices,
rapid articulation, and animated gestures. In the midst of
their violent contentions, you every moment expect they will
seize each other by the throat, and are agreeably surprised to
hear them end in a loud laugh.

"Thus it was at Alcamo, where the streets seemed to be
in an uproar till after midnight, when singing and music
began ; yet, as early as three in the morning, the people were
going about, crying aloud the bread and meat, which they sold
to the workmen that were preparing for their labour in the
fields. The Sicilians, like the Italians, need but little sleep,
and willingly part with that little for any diversion ; hence the
custom of serenading ever has and ever will prevail. Horace,
in the ninth ode of his first book, speaks of the serenades of
his days. He has been, hitherto, misinterpreted by some
commentators ; and, although the manners of the south of
Italy and of Sicily might have pointed out what the poet
intended to describe, yet I should probably still have misunder-
stood him, if a lucky accident had not informed me of the true
meaning of the verse.

"A volume of the *Gazette Littéraire de l'Europe* fell into
my hands at Naples, a journal which gave extracts from the
commentator, Abbate Galiana, a writer who died some years
ago at Naples, a man of understanding, and famous for his
numerous works. I do not believe that the whole of his com-
mentary has yet been made public.

"The ode of which I am speaking begins—

> ' Vides ut alta stet nive candidum
> Soracte.'
> —HORACE, l. i. Od. 9.

> ' Behold Soracte's airy height,
> Made heavy with a weight of snow.'
> — FRANCIS.

" The verses

' Lenesque sub noctem susurri
Composita repetantur hora.'

' An assignation sweetly made,
With gentle whispers in the dark.'

—FRANCIS.

have generally been understood as if the poet spoke of social friends who met together in the evening. But why should they speak in whispers? And why at an appointed hour? Is not the unexpected visit of a friend often the most pleasant?

" Others came nearer to the meaning, without attaining it. They supposed the poet had spoken of two lovers conversing together. Let us hear our acute Neapolitan.

" ' These *lenes susurri*,' says Galiana, ' are not the soft whispers of two lovers; they are serenades. To elucidate my meaning, it will be necessary for me to enlarge a little on the manners of the ancient Romans—manners which are still preserved in the lower parts of Italy, Spain, and the East. Love, that ever powerful, but ever hypocritical passion, suffers itself to be fettered and constrained as long as it can endure; but when it gathers sufficient strength, it breaks its chains and recovers its freedom. In Spain and Italy, where the climate will permit, the lover declares his passion in the street and at the windows. In France and Germany, where the winds are more rude, love is obliged to open the door, and tell his tale by the fire-side. In the country of Horace, the door was impassable and the house considered as sacred, particularly if it contained a young maiden that was marriageable.

" ' But let us not deceive ourselves : neither Arab nor Turk first introduced the jealousy of the seraglio to Greece and Asia. The custom is much older; it is attached to the soil, it still exists in Italy, or rather did exist, till, at the end of the last century, French manners prevailed all over Italy. In the south, however, this ancient custom still remains in full force; * the doors there are yet impassable to lovers. Watched as they are in Turkey, the girls spend a great part of their time at the window, especially by night, listening to the songs which the lovers sing in a low voice, that they may not disturb the neighbourhood. The maiden conceals the light of her chamber, and her lover only knows that she is present by her soft whispers which he hears from the balcony. I have a thousand times witnessed the scenes which Horace describes. On a sudden the girl is silent, and returns no more answers to the discourse of her lover, who, being in the dark, knows not whether she still listens or is gone. He speaks again, again waits to hear, and at last receiving no reply, is persuaded that his beloved is retired to rest; or that, frightened by a noise in her mother's chamber, she has thrown herself under the bed-clothes and counterfeited sleep.

" ' These accidents of fright are so common that the lover is not astonished if he be suddenly left in the middle of his nightly colloquy. Dejected, he puts his mandoline in its case, and is about to be gone, when, in an instant, his young mistress, who had retired to a corner of her chamber, gives a loud laugh to inform him that she still listens, and that she had only been sportively playing him a trick. Overjoyed, enraptured, he returns, and again begins his amorous endless tale.

* " This extreme restraint originates in a mistrust of women, and the ill opinion which prevails of the sex. A prudent and chaste education honours and ennobles the fair, who are most injuriously debased by oriental confinement. The German and English women are the most virtuous of their sex. Nowhere are unmarried women so innocent, or the married so happy. Nowhere are wives so honoured, and so full of worth, as among the Germans and the English. Neither have our women that cold reserve which is frequently the lot of an Englishwoman. What Galiana says of the hypocrisy of love is in part explained by the text, and in part must be understood only of this passion in the South."

" ' This agrees with the description of Horace :—

" Nunc et latentis proditor intimo
Gratus puellæ risus ab angulo :
Pignusque dereptum lacertis,
Aut digito male pertinaci."

" The laugh that from the corner flies,
The sportive fair one shall betray ;
Then boldly snatch the joyful prize,
A ring or bracelet tear away :
While she, not too severely coy,
Struggling shall yield the willing toy."
—FRANCIS.

" ' In the last two lines, Horace gives us a picture of what happens at a house door. In Italy the young girls are permitted to step to the door for a moment, especially at the beginning of night. The lover is careful to pass and repass, that he may catch the instant in which he may remind his mistress of the hour of their nightly meetings, press her to observe her promise, and endeavour to obtain a token. The last is generally no more than a pretext that he may squeeze her hand, and take a ring from her finger which is weakly defended.'

" Thus far Galiana, and I have no difficulty in admitting that the two last lines explain what actually happens. The girl has played tricks with and laughed at her lover ; and, being inclined to be reconciled, runs down to the house door. She quarrels with him only for the pleasure of making it up. Our vetturino, a lively young man, who has several times travelled over all Sicily, was not so weary by riding in the heat, but that he willingly touched the strings of his instrument nightly before many a window."—STOLBERG'S *Travels*, vol. iii. p. 447.

" We are just returned from the prince's" (the Prince of Villafranca).* " He received us politely, but with a good deal of state. He offered us the use of his carriages, as there are none to be hired ; and, in the usual style, begged to know in what he could be of service to us. We told him (with an apology for our abrupt departure) that we were obliged to set off to-morrow, and begged his protection on our journey. He replied that he would immediately give orders for guards to attend us, that should be answerable for everything ; that we need give ourselves no further trouble ; that whatever number of mules we had occasion for should be ready at the door of the inn, at any hour we should think proper to appoint. He added that we might entirely rely on these guards, who were people of the most determined resolution, as well as of the most approved confidence, and would not fail to chastise on the spot any person that should presume to impose upon us.

"Now, who do you think these trusty and well-beloved guards are composed of ? Why, of the most daring and most hardened villains, perhaps, that are to be met with upon earth, who, in any other country, would have been broken upon the wheel, or hung in chains, but are here publicly protected, and uni-versally feared and respected. It was this part of the police of Sicily that I was afraid to give you an account of. How-ever, I have now conversed with the prince's people on the subject, and they have confirmed every circumstance that Mr. Maestre made me acquainted with.

" He told me, that in this east part of the island, called Val Demoni, from the devils that are supposed to inhabit Mount Ætna, it has ever been found altogether impracticable to extirpate

---

* Probably the one mentioned in the list of Meli's subscribers.

the banditti; there being numberless caverns and subterraneous passages around that mountain, where no troops could possibly pursue them. That, besides, as they are known to be perfectly determined and resolute, never failing to take a dreadful revenge on all who have offended them, the Prince of Villafranca has embraced it, not only as the safest, but likewise as the wisest and most political scheme, to become their declared patron and protector. And such of them as think proper to leave their mountains and forests, though perhaps only for a time, are sure to meet with good encouragement, and a certain protection in his service, where they enjoy the most unbounded confidence, which, in no instance, they have ever yet been found to make an improper or a dishonest use of. They are clothed in the prince's livery, yellow and green, with silver lace, and wear likewise a badge of their honourable order, which entitles them to universal fear and respect from the people.

" I have just been interrupted by an upper servant of the prince's, who, both by his looks and language, seems to be of the same worthy fraternity. He tells us, that he has ordered our muleteers, at their peril, to be ready by daybreak; but that we need not go till we think proper : for it is their business to attend on *nostre eccellenze*. He says he has likewise ordered two of the most desperate fellows in the whole island to accompany us; adding, in a sort of whisper, that we need be under no apprehension, for that if any person should presume to impose upon us a single baiocc,* they would certainly put him to death. I gave him an ounce,† which I knew was what he expected, on which he redoubled his bows, and his eccellenzas, and declared we were the most *honorabili Signori* he had ever met with, and that, if we pleased, he himself should have the honour of attending us, and would chastise any person that should dare to take the wall of us, or injure us in the most minute trifle. We thanked him for his zeal, showing him we

---

* A small coin. † About eleven shillings.

had swords of our own. On which, bowing respectfully, he retired.

" I can now, with more assurance, give you some account of the conversation I had with Signor Maestre, who seems to be a very intelligent man, and has resided here for these great many years.

" He says that in some circumstances these banditti are the most respectable people of the island; and have by much the highest and most romantic notions of what they call their point of honour. That, however criminal they may be with regard to society in general, yet, with respect to one another, and to every person to whom they have once professed it, they have ever maintained the most unshaken fidelity. The magistrates have often been obliged to protect them, and pay them court, as they are known to be perfectly determined and desperate, and so extremely vindictive, that they will certainly put any person to death that has ever given them just cause of provocation. On the other hand, it never was known that any person who had put himself under their protection, and showed that he had confidence in them, had cause to repent of it, or was injured by any of them, in the most minute trifle ; but on the contrary, they will protect him from impositions of every kind, and scorn to go halves with the landlord, like most other conductors and travelling servants ; and will defend him with their lives, if there is occasion : that those of their number who have thus enlisted themselves in the service of society, are known and respected by the other banditti all over the island ; and. the persons of those they accompany are ever held sacred. For these reasons, most travellers choose to hire a couple of them from town to town ; and may thus travel over the whole island in safety. To illustrate their character the more, he added two stories, which happened but a few days ago, and are still in everybody's mouth.

" A number of people were found digging in a place where some treasure was supposed to have been hid during the

17

plague. As this has been forbid under the most severe penalties, they were immediately carried to prison, and expected to have been treated without mercy; but, luckily for the others, one of these heroes happened to be of the number. He immediately wrote to the Prince of Villafranca, and made use of such powerful arguments in their favour, that they were all immediately set at liberty.

" This will serve to show their consequence with the civil power. The other story will give you a strong idea of their barbarous ferocity, and the horrid mixture of stubborn vice and virtue (if I may call it by that name) that seems to direct their actions. I should have mentioned, that they have a practice of borrowing money from the country people, who never dare refuse them; and if they promise to pay it, they have ever been found punctual and exact, both as to the time and the sum; and would much rather rob and murder an innocent person, than fail of payment on the day appointed. And this they have often been obliged to do, only in order, as they say, to fulfil their engagements, and to save their honour.

" It happened within this fortnight that the brother of one of these heroic banditti having occasion for money, and not knowing how to procure it, determined to make use of his brother's name and authority, an artifice which he thought could not easily be discovered; accordingly he went to a country priest, and told him his brother had occasion for twenty ducats, which he desired he would immediately lend him. The priest assured him that he had not so large a sum, but that if he would return in a few days it should be ready for him. The other replied that he was afraid to return to his brother with this answer, and desired that he would by all means take care to keep out of his way—at least till such time as he had pacified him, otherwise he could not be answerable for the consequences. As bad fortune would have it, the very next day the priest and the robber met in a narrow road; the former fell a-trembling as the latter approached, and at last dropped on his knees to beg for mercy. The robber, astonished at this behaviour, desired to know the cause of it. The trembling priest answered, ' Il denaro, il denaro. The money —the money ; but send your brother to morrow, and you shall have it.' The haughty robber assured him that he disdained taking money of a poor priest; adding, that if any of his brothers had been low enough to make such a demand, he himself was ready to advance the sum. The priest acquainted him with the visit he had received the preceding night from his brother, by his order, assuring him, that if he had been master of the sum, he should immediately have supplied it. ' Well,' says the robber, ' I will now convince you whether my brother or I are most to be believed ; you shall go with me to his house, which is but a few miles distant.' On their arrival before the door the robber called on his brother, who, never suspecting the discovery, immediately came to the balcony ; but on perceiving the priest he began to make excuses for his conduct. The robber told him there was no excuse to be made, that he only desired to know the fact, if he had gone to borrow money of that priest in his name or not ? On his owning it, the robber with deliberate coolness lifted his blunderbuss to his shoulder and shot him dead, and turning to the astonished priest, ' You will now be persuaded,' said he, ' that I had no intention of robbing you at least.'

" You may now judge how happy we must be in company of our guards. I don't know but this very hero may be one of them."—BRYDONE's *Tour through Sicily and Malta*, vol. i. (first edition), p. 67.

GOOD-NATURED HOSPITALITY, AND FACETIOUS IGNORANT OLD GENTLEMAN.

(CHRISTMAS DAY, 1777.)

"Having spent the best part of the day in examining, measuring, and drawing this noble building, I hastened back to Calatafimi, as eager for refreshment as I had been in the morning for antiquities. I found the best fare provided for me the place could afford ; the lodging, however, was old, crazy, and cold, but the owners so civil and attentive that it was impossible to complain of any inconveniences; the master of the house was a notary, and his wife one of the prettiest women I had yet seen in Sicily. I was afterwards distressed beyond measure to learn that they had not suffered my man to pay for the least thing, and had sitten up all night to accommodate us with beds. To enliven the evening conversation they invited the principal people of the town with their wives, who were very free and sociable ; this rather surprised me, as many travellers, and those very modern ones, tell us that the Sicilians are so jealous and severe to their wives that they never suffer them to come into the company of strangers, much less to join in conversation with them. I suspect these persons have copied authors who wrote in times when such mistrust reigned more than it does at present, or have formed general inductions from partial evidence. There seems to be very little constraint laid upon the intercourse of the two sexes among the nobility at Palermo, and none among my visitors at Calatafimi, people of a lower class ; the observation, therefore, does not hold good in every instance. The assembly was very attentive to all my words and motions, that they might anticipate my wishes and save me trouble ; but their civility was of an unpolished kind. I was frequently the subject of their discourse, and those that knew anything about me, either from the archbishop's letter or from my servants, communicated their knowledge aloud to every new-comer, as if I were deaf or did not understand their language. An old gentleman, the wit of the circle, put many questions to me, and in return acquainted me with the politics and scandal of the town. He was possessed of great cheerfulness and native humour, but so totally ignorant of every thing and place beyond the limits of Sicily, that I never could make him comprehend where England is situated, or how circumstanced with regard to its colonies, of which he has learned something from the gazettes. Finding my answers to his questions were incapable of conveying instruction, I gave myself no farther trouble, but suffered him without interruption to smoke his pipe, and in the intervals of his puffing to run on in a long string of stories, confounding times, names, places, and persons, in so ridiculous a manner, that the most inflexible features must have been betrayed into a smile : fortunately he took my laugh for a compliment, and joined very heartily in it."—SWINBURNE's *Travels in the Two Sicilies*, vol. iii p. 357.

SPECIMEN OF HIGHER SOCIETY.

" WILD honey is found in great abundance in these woods " (between Terranova and Calatagerone), " but the inhabitants have also hives near their houses ; its flavour is delicious, and has been celebrated from the remotest antiquity, for Hybla was situated in the centre of this country. Men may degenerate, may forget the arts by which they acquired renown ; manufactures may fail, and commodities be debased ; but the sweets of the wild-flowers of the wilderness, the industry and natural mechanics of the bee, will continue without change or derogation. From the quality of soil, and the want of water, this upper part of the province must always have had a great deal of waste land.

"The corn wore the most promising appearance : the fallow land seemed to be excellent soil. Twenty-three pair of oxen were ploughing together within a square of thirty acres.

"Beyond the town we entered a very fine tract of vineyards, which improved as we gradually approached the mountains of Calatagerone.

"Calatagerone, a royal city, containing about 17,000 inhabitants, living by agriculture and the making of potter's ware, is twenty miles from the sea, and situated on the summit of a very high, insulated hill, embosomed in thick groves of cypresses; the road to it, though paved, is very steep, difficult, and dangerous for anything but a mule or an ass. I was conducted to the college of the late Jesuits; and as the house was completely stripped of furniture, full of dirt and cobwebs, I apprehended my night's lodgings would be but indifferent. The servant belonging to the gentleman who has the management of this forfeited estate, and to whom I had brought a letter requesting a lodging in the college, perceiving the difficulties we lay under in making our settlement, ran home, and returned in a short time with a polite invitation to his master's house. There was no refusing such an offer, though I was far from expecting anything beyond a comfortable apartment and homely fare in a family settled among the inland mountains of Sicily ; but, to my great surprise, I found the house of the Baron of Rosabia large, convenient, and fitted up in a modern taste with furniture that would be deemed elegant in any capital city in Europe. Everything suited this outward show, attendance, table, plate, and equipage. The baron and his lady having both travelled and seen a great deal of the world, had returned to settle in their native city, where they assured me I might find many families equally improved by an acquaintance with the manners of foreign countries, or at least a frequentation of the best company in their own metropolis. Nothing could be more easy and polite than their address and conversation, and my astonishment was hourly increasing during my whole stay. After I had refreshed myself with a short but excellent meal, they took me out in a very handsome coach. It was a singular circumstance to meet a string of carriages full of well-dressed ladies and gentlemen on the summit of a mountain which no vehicle can ascend, unless it be previously taken to pieces and placed upon the back of mules. We seemed to be seated among the clouds. As the vast expanse of the hills and vales grew dim with the evening vapours, our parading resembled the amusements of the heathen gods in some poems and pictures, driving about Olympus, and looking down at the mortals below.

"The hour of airing being expired, which consisted of six turns of about half a mile each, a numerous assembly was formed at the baron's house; the manners of the company were extremely polished, and the French language familiar to the greatest part of it. When the card-tables were removed, a handsome supper, dressed by a French cook, was served up, with excellent foreign and Sicilian wines; the conversation took a lively turn, and was well supported till midnight, when we all retired to rest. Calatagerone has several houses that live in the same elegant style, and its inhabitants have the reputation of being the politest people in the island."— SWINBURNE's *Travels*, vol. iii. p. 337.

POETICAL TURN OF THE SICILIANS.

"NEXT to the lava-labours of Ætna, nothing has struck me more in this beautiful island than the poetical turn of the people. *Theocritus* was the father of Idylls; and *Virgil* is always appealing to the ' Sicelides Musæ.' I suspect the experience detailed in his *Georgics*, his most perfect work, was most mainly drawn from hence. The words ' Calabri rapuêre ' in the epitaph attributed to him for his own tomb, whether they were really his or no, prove, by inference, that he was close opposite this coast at the most observant period of life; and no doubt he crossed over. *Dante* allows that the first Italian effusions in playful satire were termed ' Siciliani.' Even *Petrarch* savours of Trinacria. The speech of the inhabitants is to this day rather poetical than prosaic, abounding in lively images and picturesque modes of expression. The studied cringing so common in Naples is rare here : during a stay of six weeks in the island, I have only twice heard the title ' Cellenza,' which is everlastingly ringing in your ears in the metropolis. Their similitudes are endless, and sometimes very striking. In Florence you will hear ' Bello come il campanile ' (' as handsome as the belfry,'—built by Giotto): but here, if a lady is fair, she is ' una candela di cera ' (' a wax taper '); if too languid, ' ha un viso come un pesce bollito ' (' has a face like a boiled fish '); gentlemen who sit sluggishly on their mules instead of springing off to aid the weaker sex up the hill, are designated as ' pezzi di lava ' (' lumps of lava '). If a little girl has anything remarkable about her, ' È molto simpatica, una cosa particolare ' (' She is very sympathetic ;—a special sort of thing '). ' Buscar qualche cosa ' (' to look for something '), I am sorry to say, has here, as in Ischia, the double meaning, either to earn a carline or steal it, as the case may be. Their humour is never richer than when shown in describing their own peculiarities of character.—*Notes from a Journal kept in Italy and Sicily, by* J. F. FRANCIS, B.A.

A MEETING OF ENGLISH AND SICILIAN DISHES ON CHRISTMAS DAY.

"We paid a visit to Messina a week ago, where we had the pleasure of being wind-bound on Christmas day. In merry England on Christmas day people eat roast beef and plum-pudding, turkeys and mince-pies. You may eat most of these here also, but the special dish in honour of the 'Natività' is *capitoni*, enormous eels, stewed in a rich sauce. Indeed there was an unusual supply, for a shipload of them, intended for the Naples market, could not leave port in time owing to the gale, and thus the speculator, a sea-captain, was fain to get rid of them in Messina at half-price. Now I can only say they are very good; but we took the precaution of having another string to our bow, in shape of a respectable roast joint of beef, and a real, good, English-looking plum-pudding. After that it is very hard if we are left for the year of grace 'eighteen forty-six' without Victoria's bonny face in our purse."—Francis' *Notes*, p. 240.

THE END.

LONDON : PRINTED BY
SPOTTISWOODE AND CO., NEW-STREET SQUARE
AND PARLIAMENT STREET